How to Make a Mummy Talk

Lindow Man

How to Make a Mummy Talk

James M. Deem

Illustrated by True Kelley

A Yearling Book

Published by
Bantam Doubleday Dell Books for Young Readers
a division of
Bantam Doubleday Dell Publishing Group, Inc.
1540 Broadway
New York, New York 10036

The poem "Baby Mummy" from *The Wetherills of Mesa Verde* (Cranbury, New Jersey: Associated University Presses, 1977) by Benjamin Alfred Wetherill, edited and annotated by Maurine S. Fletcher, is reprinted by permission of Roger C. Fletcher.

ISBN: 0-440-41316-8

Reprinted by arrangement with Houghton Mifflin Company

Printed in the United States of America

July 1997

10 9 8 7 6 5 4 3 2

CWO

For Manny and Muriel,
mummy master and master mummy

OTHER YEARLING BOOKS YOU WILL ENJOY:

HOW TO READ YOUR MOTHER'S MIND, *James M. Deem*
EARTH TO MATTHEW, *Paula Danziger*
EVERYONE ELSE'S PARENTS SAID YES, *Paula Danziger*
MAKE LIKE A TREE AND LEAVE, *Paula Danziger*
NOT FOR A BILLION GAZILLION DOLLARS, *Paula Danziger*
BE A PERFECT PERSON IN JUST THREE DAYS!, *Stephen Manes*
MAKE FOUR MILLION DOLLARS BY NEXT THURSDAY!, *Stephen Manes*
HOW TO EAT FRIED WORMS, *Thomas Rockwell*
HOW TO FIGHT A GIRL, *Thomas Rockwell*
HOW TO GET FABULOUSLY RICH, *Thomas Rockwell*

YEARLING BOOKS are designed especially to entertain and enlighten young people. Patricia Reilly Giff, consultant to this series, received her bachelor's degree from Marymount College and a master's degree in history from St. John's University. She holds a Professional Diploma in Reading and a Doctorate of Humane Letters from Hofstra University. She was a teacher and reading consultant for many years, and is the author of numerous books for young readers.

For a complete listing of all Yearling titles, write to
Dell Readers Service,
P.O. Box 1045
South Holland, IL 60473

Contents

A Few Words about Mummies

Mummies are an endangered species. Long taken for granted and sometimes misused or even abused, they have begun to disappear from many museums worldwide. Supernatural forces are not the cause. Rather, two earthly reasons explain their disappearance. Sometimes, mummies have been removed from exhibit because they have literally fallen apart from age or the conditions in poorly ventilated or insect-ridden display cases. Often, mummies have been taken from public view when people — including the descendants of the mummies — have questioned the need to exhibit dead people.

And who can blame them? In the past, the mummies of indigenous peoples (such as Native Americans or the Guanches from the Canary Islands) were displayed as curiosities, with little or no respect for the mummy or its present or past relatives. And scientists were often as much to blame as the owners of carnival sideshows.

Mummies are still a fascinating subject, and most people are curious about them. But mummies are much more than freaks and curiosities. They are not strange, gross, or even unpleasant. They are, many believe, time capsules that allow today's scientists and others to peer back into the past to see what life was like. In order to avoid the sensationalism of the past, this book does not contain any photographs of mummies. Instead, you will find detailed stories, enlivened by illustrations, about the lives and deaths of people and animals who became mummies. You may be able to find photos of these mummies in other books. The point is not what they looked like, however, but how they lived, how they died, and what we can learn about them and the worlds they inhabited.

Egyptian Professional Mourners

Introduction

Have you ever looked at a mummy and wondered how it was made and where it came from? Did you picture what kind of life it lived and how it died? Did you imagine the stories it might tell you — if only it could talk?

How to Make a Mummy Talk will take you on a tour of mummies worldwide and explain why scientists have not had to wait for the miracle of a talking mummy. Without speaking, mummies have still managed to share many of their secrets. Part One discusses what mummies are, how they are created, and where they have been found. Part Two illustrates the careful and nondestructive steps scientists must take when they investigate mummies and their mysteries. Part Three explains why and how mummies (of any age and from any society) should be treated with respect. Along the way, you'll meet some mummy dummies (that is, people who have mistreated mummies) and some mummy masters. I've also included Mummy Finders that pinpoint the location of mummies still on exhibit at various museums.

Throughout the book, you will read the true stories of mummies that have been discovered around the world. Some of the human ones met very unpleasant deaths. If this scares you, remember that no matter what movies or other books may lead you to believe, they will not be coming back to life — except in your imagination. And many of the civilizations that practiced mummification used strange and sometimes hard-to-stomach procedures. Try not to be shocked when you read these descriptions. Rather, allow yourself to understand why many civilizations employed such practices when it came to burying and/or preserving their dead.

Finally, a note about my use of the word "mummy." Many Egyptologists (that is, scientists who study ancient Egypt) prefer to use the word "mummy" only to refer to the intentional process used by the Egyptians. Other scientists use the word to refer to all preserved bodies, intentional or accidental, Egyptian or not. In this book, I have chosen to use the word in this more inclusive way.

If you'd like to share your ideas about or any experiences with mummies, please write to me at the following address: James M. Deem, ℅ Houghton Mifflin Company, 222 Berkeley Street, Boston, Massachusetts 02116.

Here's hoping that you meet many mummies on your way to becoming a mummy master.

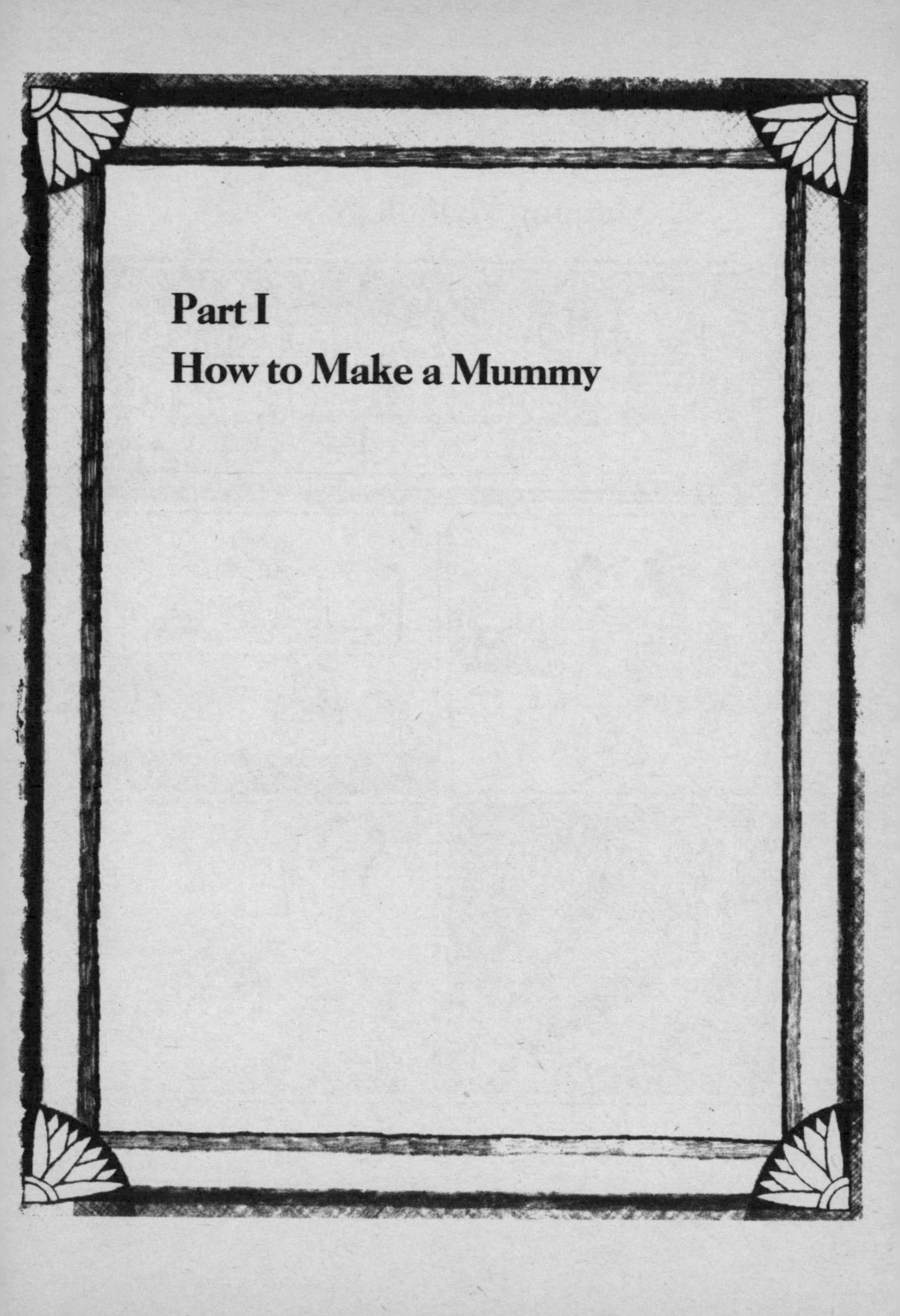

Part I
How to Make a Mummy

1. Mummy Mythology

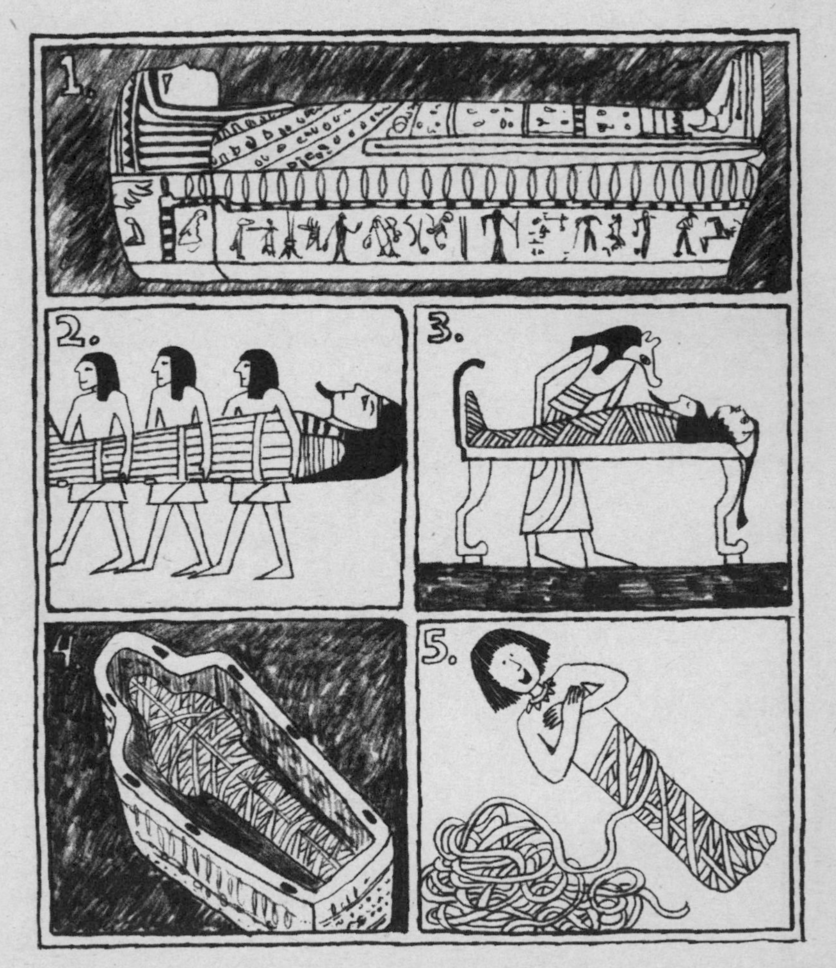

What do you know about mummies? Before you can learn how scientists have made mummies talk, you need to know the facts about them. Test your knowledge on the following questions:

The Mummy Mythology Test

Answer true or false to each of the following statements.

1. Almost all mummies come from Egypt.
2. Mummies were first made in Egypt.
3. Mummies were always created by mummymakers.
4. Mummies are always wrapped in linen, put in beautiful coffins, and buried in old tombs.
5. If their wrappings are removed, most Egyptian mummies look as if they are alive.
6. Only people can become mummies.
7. There is only one way to make a mummy.
8. Anyone who finds a mummy will be cursed.
9. Mummies were made to scare people.
10. All mummies are hundreds or thousands of years old.

Now turn the page to find the correct answers.

Answers: All of the statements are false.
This chapter and the next will explain why.

Don't be surprised if your ideas have been clouded by some misconceptions. Many people have mistaken ideas about mummies, because very little comprehensive information exists. When researchers discover a new mummy or analyze one already found, they do not register it with a Central Mummy Office. Therefore, determining which mummy is the world's oldest or best preserved is virtually impossible. There is no list of all the mummies ever found, let alone all the mummies on display in the world's museums, to help them. What's more, very few scientists actually study mummies. Those who do almost always specialize in studying human mummies from a particular civilization; they often have little interest in comparing them to mummies from other societies. It's no wonder, then, that quite a few mummy myths have developed.

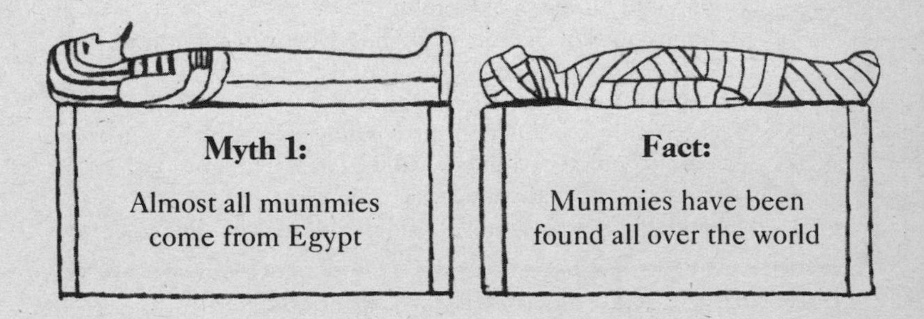

Myth 1:
Almost all mummies come from Egypt
Fact:
Mummies have been found all over the world

Most people think of mummies as Egyptian, and with good reason. From about 2600 B.C. to A.D. 641, Egyptians deliberately mummified their dead, creating millions of mummies. Because they made so many mummies over such a long period of time and because they often used excellent mummymaking techniques, Egyptian mummies have easily become the most famous in the world.

But other civilizations around the world also preserved their dead. According to mummy expert Aidan Cockburn, millions of other mummies also exist. In fact, human mummies have been discovered on every inhabited continent, including North America. Even Antarctica, where the cold temperatures freeze-dry anything that dies there, has yielded a large number of seal mummies, some thousands of years old.

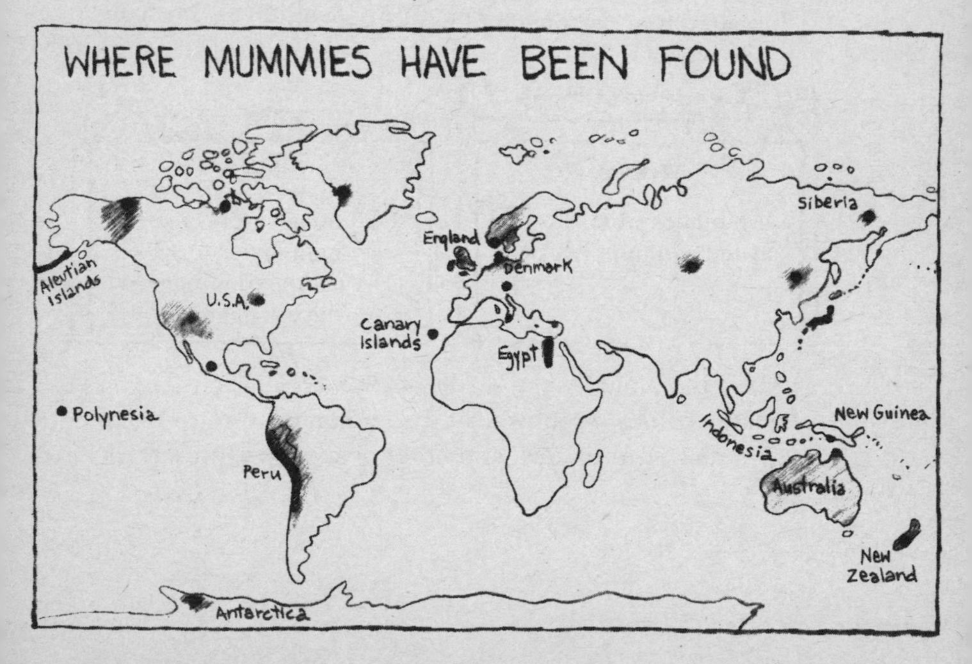

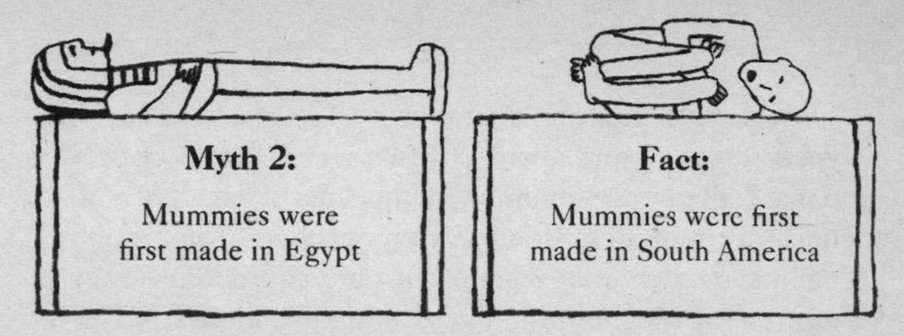

Myth 2:
Mummies were
first made in Egypt
Fact:
Mummies were first
made in South America

Although Egyptian mummies are the best known, they are not the oldest. Rather, the oldest human mummies made by mummymakers have been found in South America, and they are about 5,000–7,000 years old. This fact, though, could change as anthropologists and archaeologists discover more mummified remains around the world. Some anthropologists suspect that native tribes from Australia, Papua New Guinea, and the islands that lie between them may have practiced mummification as long as 9,000 years ago. One day, therefore, the oldest human mummies may be found there.

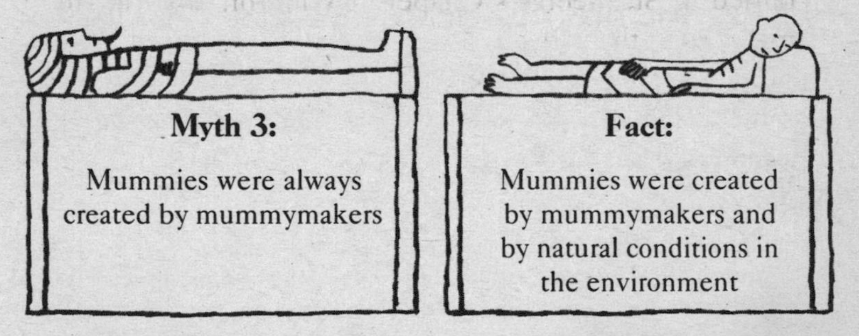

Myth 3:
Mummies were always
created by mummymakers
Fact:
Mummies were created
by mummymakers and
by natural conditions in
the environment

Most mummies were made *intentionally;* that is, upon death, bodies were prepared in a certain way to make sure that skin, tissues, and other organs were preserved.

Sometimes, however, mummies were made *accidentally* or naturally, because of the type of place in which a body was buried.

Some civilizations practiced intentional mummification. A few may have mummified almost everyone who died; the Egyptians eventually did this. Others concentrated on mummifying their leaders. For example, Incan kings and their families were preserved, as were the kings and princes of Austria, Cockburn says. The body of the Russian leader Vladimir Lenin was also mummified and displayed in a tomb in Moscow for many years, perhaps to show that his ideas continued to live after his death.

Sometimes, though, accidental mummies were created. King Charles I of England, who was beheaded in 1648, reportedly became an accidental mummy while buried in St. George's Chapel in Windsor. In 1813, to make sure that Charles was indeed buried there, his coffin was opened. Sir Henry Halford, who was present at the examination, described what he saw when the decapitated head was removed:

> The complexion of the skin was dark and discolored. The forehead and temples had lost little or nothing of their muscular substance; the cartilage of the nose was gone; but the left eye, in the first moment of exposure, was open and full, though it vanished almost immediately: and the pointed beard, so characteristic of this period of the reign of King Charles, was perfect.

> [The head] was quite wet, and gave a greenish-red tinge to paper and to linen which touched it. The back part of the scalp . . . had a remarkably fresh appearance. . . . The hair was thick . . . and in appearance nearly black. . . . On the back part of the head it was not more than an inch in length and had probably been cut so short for the convenience of the executioner, or perhaps . . . to furnish memorials of the unhappy king.

On September 19, 1991, a different type of accidental mummy was discovered on the border of Italy and Austria in the Tyrolean Alps. Erika and Helmut Simon, who were on a mountain-climbing vacation, saw a body lying face down in some ice. They assumed, as did the local authorities, that they had found the mummified remains of a mountain climber. It is sometimes difficult to recover the body of a fallen climber, especially if a fresh snowfall covers the area. The body freezes and does not deteriorate; many such mummies have been recovered.

For this reason, "rescuers" made quite a few mistakes. At first, using sticks that they found nearby, they attempted to pry him free. They also tried to pull him from the ice by grabbing on to what was left of his clothing. In the process, they shredded it. One policeman was so anxious to free the mummy that he took a jackhammer to the ice, accidentally drilling a hole in the mummy's hip.

When he was finally freed, the mummy was forced into a coffin, which caused his left arm to break. Then, according to author David Roberts, when photographers were given time to take pictures of the mummy in a nearby morgue, a fungus spread across the mummy's skin.

In the end, Italian and Austrian authorities were shocked to discover that rather than being a modern-day mountain climber, the man had died about 3000 B.C. He quickly came to be known as the Iceman, one of the oldest and best preserved human mummies ever found, according to many researchers.

Most interesting to scientists was the wealth of possessions that the Iceman carried. These included a copper ax that, amazingly, had its bindings and handle still attached. They also found his tool kit, which included a dagger with a flint blade, a bone needle, and a piece of grass rope. He also had twelve untipped arrows and a bow that the rescuers had unknowingly used to pry the Iceman loose.

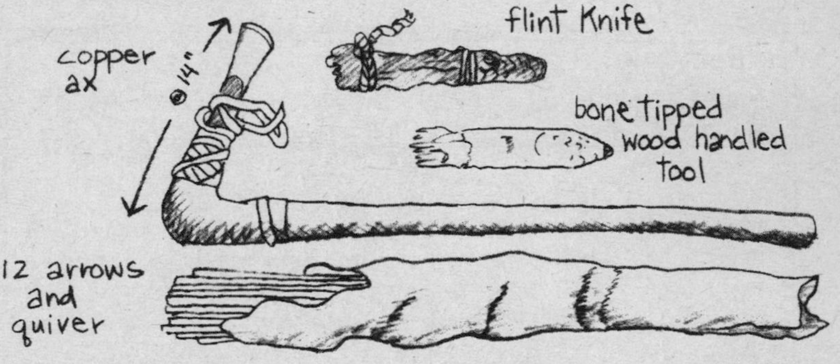

Although researchers have many questions about the Iceman, they are unable to study his body for long periods of time, for fear that his condition will deteriorate. They know that he was five feet two inches tall, weighed 110 pounds, and wore the equivalent of a size six leather boot. He also had shoulder-length brown hair and geometric tattoos on his knees, ankles, and back. They concluded that he was between twenty-five and forty years old when he died and that he might have died from exhaustion. He is thought to have been a shepherd or trader, but no one knows for certain who he was or what he was doing in the mountains.

In late August 1992, author Torstein Sjøvold climbed to the 10,000-foot site where the Iceman's mummy was found. Even though he had used a modern path part of the way, he found the climb grueling. Suddenly, fog enveloped him; the temperature dropped below freezing. He couldn't continue his climb until the fog lifted. When it did, he went on to a nearby lodge. That night, the first heavy snow of the year fell in the mountains.

Sjøvold wondered if the same events might have happened to the Copper Age man five thousand years earlier:

> If he had just climbed to the top of the mountain passage, he would have been quite tired. He might then have been caught in a fog, lain down, and fallen asleep while waiting for the fog to dissipate. If later on it started to snow, he could have been chilled and, remaining unconscious, fallen into his eternal sleep.

With further study, the Iceman may reveal many more answers.

MUMMY FINDER: The Iceman is not presently on exhibit. In cold storage at the University of Innsbruck, Austria, he is being examined slowly and carefully to make sure that his body is preserved. Eventually, he will be returned to Italy where he may be displayed in an archaeology museum in the Bolzano province.

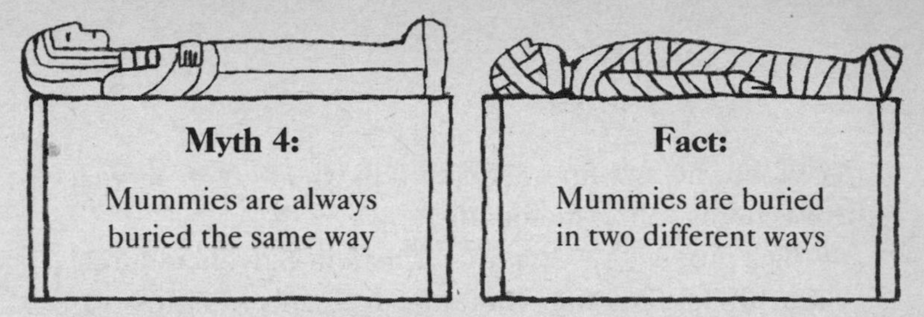

Myth 4:
Mummies are always buried the same way
Fact:
Mummies are buried in two different ways

People generally visualize mummies wrapped in linen bandages, fitted into decorated coffins, and hidden in dusty tombs. Numerous movies and books have portrayed mummies in exactly this way.

Although it is true that many intentional Egyptian mummies look like this, some were wrapped only in a reed mat. As for accidental mummies and most intentional mummies of the world, they are buried quite differently. They may be dressed in clothes or be naked. They may be placed in tombs, put into baskets, or stretched out on large wooden platforms.

What mummies do share is the position in which they are buried. In fact, almost all mummies are found in one of two positions. Sometimes the body is *flexed*, either tightly or loosely; that is, it is drawn up into a fetal position. A tightly flexed mummy is curled up into a ball, while a loosely flexed mummy will look much more relaxed. A flexed mummy can be seated, kneeling, or

reclining. Other times the body is *extended;* that is, stretched out. For example, intentional Egyptian mummies are always in extended positions, though Egyptologist Thomas Pettigrew noted that the position of their arms can vary:

> The arms are found either lying along the sides of the body, the palms of the hands in contact with the thighs, or placed upon the groins, or brought forward in contact with each other, or they are placed across the breast, or, as in some rare instances, one arm extended along the side of the body, while the other is carried across the chest.

On the other hand, accidental Egyptian mummies uncovered in the sand are almost always in flexed positions.

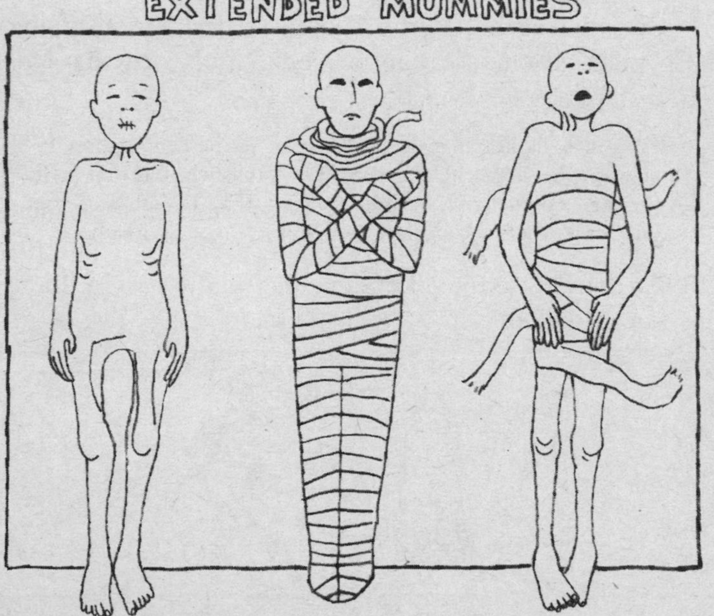

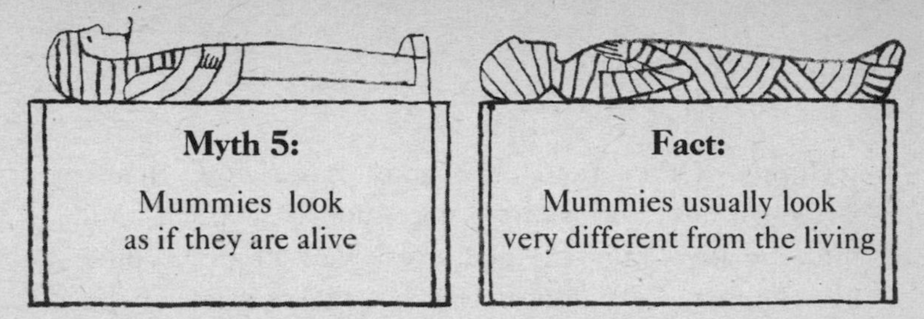

Myth 5:
Mummies look
as if they are alive
Fact:
Mummies usually look
very different from the living

Despite their differences, mummies of the world share another common trait: unwrapped or undressed, most resemble a person from which the fluids have been removed. Unless the mummy has been packed with sawdust or powder, or surrounded by liquid, the face and body will look shriveled, wrinkled, and tightly drawn. Its eyeballs will often be missing. Sometimes the skin will be soft; other times, it will be quite dry and brittle — this depends on the method that created the mummy. In other words, most human mummies do not really look like living persons.

Consider author Carol Andrews's description of the Egyptian mummification process: after forty days of preparation, a person's body

> was much darker in color and up to 75 percent lighter in weight. The arms and legs were like matchsticks but the trunk was sleeved in loose, rather rubbery skin, for most of the muscles and soft tissues had been broken down or dissolved.

This doesn't sound like someone you'd pass walking down the street.

These five myths are probably the most basic ones concerning mummies. But as you'll read in the next chapter, they are not the only ones.

The Jackal - symbol of Anubis, the Egyptian god of embalming.

2. More Mummy Mythology

Here are five more myths and facts to consider in your quest to understand the truth about mummies:

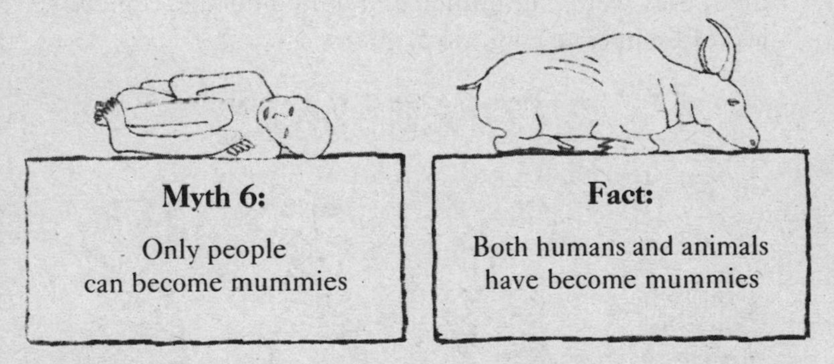

Myth 6:
Only people can become mummies
Fact:
Both humans and animals have become mummies

Mummies come in all shapes and sizes — and species. The ancient Egyptians mummified reptiles and animals such as dogs, apes, bulls, rams, and even an occasional hippopotamus. However, one of the most common animal mummies was the cat.

To determine how, when, and why cats were mummi-

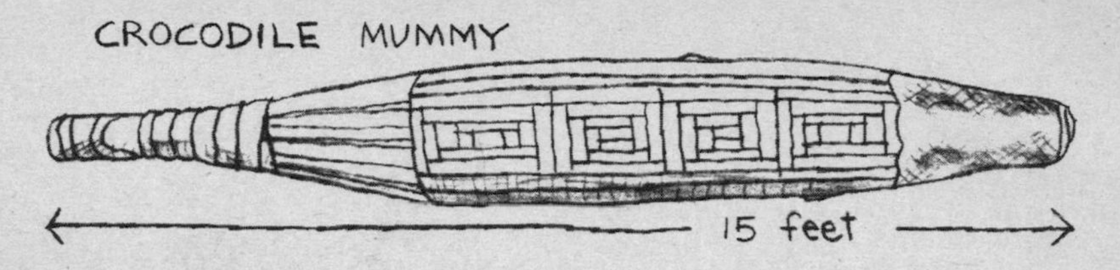

fied, Egyptologists have had to piece together many clues. It appears, for example, that by 1350 B.C. cats were occasionally buried with their owners, according to author Jaromir Malek. But by 900 B.C., a striking change had taken place in the Egyptians' religious beliefs. Many animals were now thought to be the embodiment of certain gods and goddesses; cats were believed to represent the goddess Bastet. Consequently, they were raised in and around temples devoted to Bastet. When they died, they were mummified and buried in huge cemeteries, often in large communal graves.

An even more important change took place over the centuries. From about 332 B.C. to 30 B.C., animals began to be raised for the specific purpose of being turned into mummies. The mummies were sold to people on their way to worship a god and left at the temple as offerings. Scientists have uncovered a gruesome fact: many cats died quite premature and unnatural deaths. Two- to four-month-old kittens seemed to have been sacrificed in huge numbers, perhaps, as Malek supposes, because they fit into the mummy container better. So many cat

mummies were made that researchers can only guess that there were millions of them. In fact, one company bought 38,000 pounds of cat mummies in the late 1800s to pulverize and sell as fertilizer in England; this shipment alone probably contained 180,000 mummified cats!

Accidental animal mummies have also been found, ranging from adult mammoths in Siberia to two tiny puppies from Ventana Cave that are on display in the Arizona State Museum in Tucson.

"DIMA," the Siberian baby mammoth found in 1977. One of the oldest mummies in the world - 27,000 to 40,000 years old.
4 feet tall
4 feet long
198 lbs.

One interesting animal mummy is that of a 36,000-year-old male bison, discovered just north of Fairbanks, Alaska, in July 1979. According to zoologist R. Dale Guthrie, a gold miner first noticed the mummy that came to be called Blue Babe. Using a high-pressure water gun, the miner was washing away layers of frozen silt near Pearl Creek in order to uncover a layer of gravel that contained gold, when he saw the bison's feet sticking out of the mud. He quickly reported his find to the University of Alaska, and Guthrie was sent to inspect the body.

Beginning with the Alaskan gold rush, many miners had come across the frozen mummies of large animals. Often the bodies were incomplete, and since the miners were much more interested in finding their fortunes than in exploring the past, the carcasses were set aside and left to rot. Guthrie was impressed when he saw Blue Babe for the first time; the body was almost completely intact.

Although Guthrie was anxious to study Blue Babe, he was just about to begin a year's sabbatical in Europe. This meant that Blue Babe and the frozen silt that surrounded it would have to bc placed in cold storage for a year. Fortunately, Guthrie was able to locate a huge walk-in freezer at the University of Alaska, and Blue Babe was moved there.

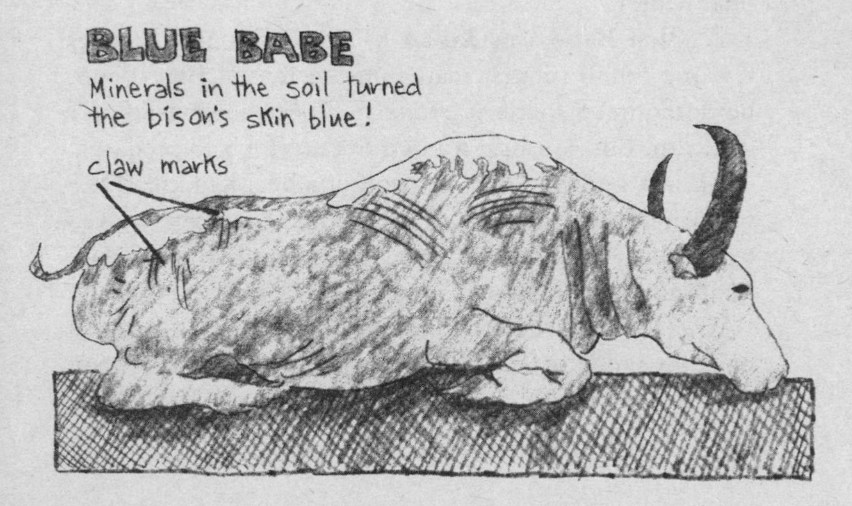

BLUE BABE
Minerals in the soil turned the bison's skin blue!
claw marks

A year later, Guthrie carefully examined the bison to determine when and how it died. His investigation uncovered a number of facts:

1. Blue Babe died in early winter. Four clues pointed to this fact. First, Blue Babe's fur was clearly a winter coat. Second, the body contained a great deal of fat, indicating that the normally lean animal was ready for winter. Third, Guthrie's analysis of Blue Babe's teeth and horns also showed that its summer growth was over. Finally, the body had been attacked and the flesh partially eaten. Since the carcass was mostly complete, Guthrie concluded that the body froze after it was only partly eaten. Guthrie explained, "When a large carcass freezes, the skin becomes almost like sheet steel; a heavy, frozen hide is difficult for a predator or scavenger to penetrate." If the bison had died in July, its body would not have been in good condition when it froze the next winter.

2. Blue Babe was killed by another animal. After Guthrie found scratch marks on the rear of Blue Babe, he determined that a predator had been responsible for its death. But, Guthrie wanted to know, which predator?

At first, he wondered if a wolf or a bear had killed the bison and made the long scratch marks. However, wolves leave much smaller scratches, and a bear (which usually hunts alone) would have been no match for the bison.

By comparing the scratches on Blue Babe to the marks made by predators, Guthrie deduced that Blue Babe had been killed by a lion. The wounds matched those found on the bodies of African buffalo killed by lions. What's more, Guthrie also found a most convincing piece of evidence — a large piece of lion's tooth buried in the bison's neck. Are you surprised that lions might once have lived in Alaska? Guthrie noted that at one time lions roamed Europe and North America. What's more, 36,000-year-old lion fossils have been discovered in Alaska.

Guthrie suspected that two or three lions killed Blue Babe and began to eat the carcass. Since the bison was too big for the lions to consume at once, they left the body for a time. Before they could return to feed again,

Guthrie hypothesized, freezing weather set in. Frozen bison meat would have been too tough for the lions, and by the time spring came, the body was buried in a flow of silt that ensured it would remain frozen and mummified.

MUMMY FINDER: Today Blue Babe is displayed at the University of Alaska in Fairbanks. But the bison on display is not exactly the same as the one pulled out of Pearl Creek. A plaster mold of the body was created, then covered with Blue Babe's tanned and treated skin. In celebration of the finished display mummy, Guthrie and his partners ate a special dinner of bison stew: "A small part of the mummy's neck was diced and simmered in a pot of stock and vegetables. We had Blue Babe for dinner. The meat was well aged but still a little tough, and it gave the stew a strong Pleistocene aroma, but nobody there would have dared miss it."

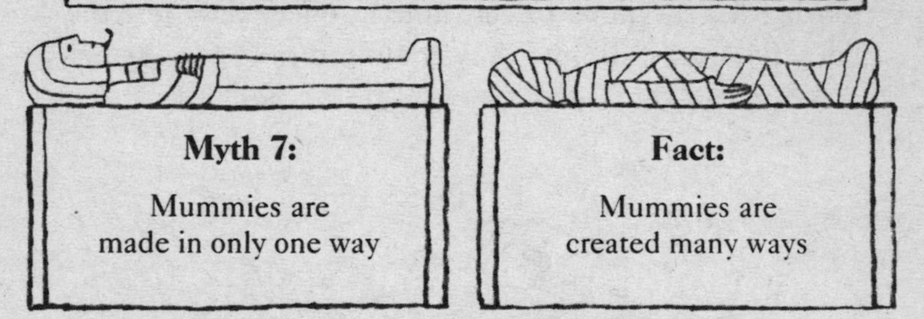

Myth 7:
Mummies are made in only one way
Fact:
Mummies are created many ways

The Egyptian method of intentional mummification is the best known. This method is a series of different techniques that changed over the course of 3,000 years. And many other methods used by different civilizations exist.

Intentional mummies may have been smoked over a fire or drained of all bodily fluid. Their internal organs may have been removed (which would stop the inside of the body from rotting) and their skin may have been treated with special substances (which would maintain the body's outer appearance). Of course, some mummies are better preserved than others, depending on the techniques used and the skill of the practitioner. On the other hand, accidental mummies were (and still are) made when a corpse is dried, frozen, or buried in ground that does not contain any air.

One unusual method of mummy creation first occurred in Japan between the years 1000–1200 B.C. Some Buddhist priests attempted to mummify themselves while they were still living. To accomplish this, the priest would go on a very strict diet for a period of three years. He would no longer eat such foods as rice, barley, or beans. As he began to lose weight, the priest would place large candles around his body and light them — in effect, the priest was drying out his body with the heat produced by the candles. By the time the priest died of starvation, his body was practically mummified. To make

Tetsumon Kai, a Japanese Buddhist priest who died in 1829 after three years on a starvation diet.

sure that mummification was complete, the body was then placed in an underground tomb for three years before being dried out, one more time, by candles.

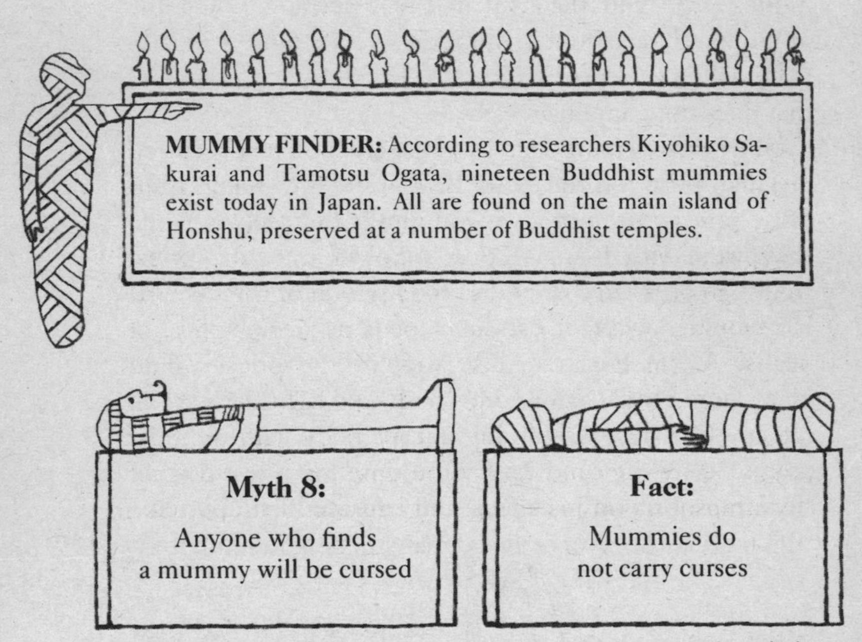

MUMMY FINDER: According to researchers Kiyohiko Sakurai and Tamotsu Ogata, nineteen Buddhist mummies exist today in Japan. All are found on the main island of Honshu, preserved at a number of Buddhist temples.

Myth 8:

Anyone who finds a mummy will be cursed

Fact:

Mummies do not carry curses

Although people are often frightened of mummies, it is untrue that finding a mummy can lead to a curse on the discoverer. Author Christine El Mahdy believes that those who first expressed fear of mummies were the Arabs, who conquered Egypt in A.D. 641. Arab writers warned people not to tamper with mummies or their tombs; they knew that Egyptians practiced magic during funerals. And the paintings on the walls of Egyptian tombs seemed to suggest that mummies could return to life and seek revenge.

The idea that mummies had magic power eventually appealed to the imaginations of authors. After the first ghost story about a mummy's curse was published in 1699, many more followed. But the longest lasting episode involving a mummy's curse was the discovery and opening of King Tutankhamen's tomb in 1923.

This story has been told many times, but fact and fiction are usually blended. Two recent authors who have separated the facts from the myths are Christopher Frayling and Nicholas Reeves.

First, the facts: Lord Carnarvon, who had funded the search for King Tut's tomb, and archaeologist Howard Carter entered the king's burial chamber on February 17, 1923. On or about March 6, Lord Carnarvon was bitten by a mosquito on his cheek and became ill. Reported in the media, this event caused many people to jump to the conclusion that King Tut's tomb was cursed.

Many famous people volunteered their theories to the press. For example, Marie Corelli, a popular novelist of the time, expressed her thoughts in a letter published in New York and London newspapers. In part, her letter read:

> I cannot but think some risks are run by breaking into the last rest of a king in Egypt whose tomb is specially and solemnly guarded, and robbing him of his possessions. According to a

rare book I possess . . . entitled *The Egyptian History of the Pyramids* [an ancient Arabic text], the most dire punishment follows any rash intruder into a sealed tomb. The book . . . names 'secret poisons enclosed in boxes in such wise that those who touch them shall not know how they come to suffer'. That is why I ask, Was it a mosquito bite that has so seriously infected Lord Carnarvon?

Corelli reported that the Egyptian author also warned: "Death comes on wings to he who enters the tomb of a pharaoh."

Her concerns seemed to be on target when Lord Carnarvon's condition worsened. The mosquito bite became infected, he contracted pneumonia, and on April 5, he died. The legend of the curse became fact and was enhanced by many rumors. Here are five of the most famous — and the real truth behind them:

Rumor 1: On the day of the tomb opening, Carnarvon's pet canary was eaten by a cobra (a symbol of the ancient pharaohs). The truth is that, although Carter had a pet canary, he gave it to a friend named Minnie Burton to watch, and she gave it (alive and well) to a bank manager.

Rumor 2: At the moment that Carnarvon died in Cairo Hospital, the lights across Cairo went out for five minutes. Actually, around the time that Carnarvon died, the *hospital* lights did go out for a few moments. Within a few weeks' time, this fact was twisted into the more interesting rumor. As Christine El Mahdy points out, the lights in Cairo are notorious for going out without warning — even today.

Rumor 3: Carnarvon's dog Susie, back in England, howled and dropped dead at exactly two o'clock in the morning, the time that Carnarvon died. No one knows whether this story is true or not, but it seems suspicious, especially since Egypt and England do not share the same time zone. The story might be a bit more believable if Susie had died at two o'clock Egyptian time.

Rumor 4: Over the door to King Tut's tomb was an

inscription that read "Death shall come on swift wings to him that toucheth the tomb of the Pharaoh." Notice that this inscription closely matches the quotation Marie Corelli cited from the ancient Arabic text. Even today, it is easy to find books that report this inscription as fact. For example, in his recent book about mummies, author John Vornholt writes, "In an outer chamber, they [Carter and Carnarvon] found a clay tablet that read: 'Death will slay with his wings whoever disturbs the peace of the Pharaoh.' " This is simply not true.

Rumor 5: Most of the people present at the opening of the tomb met untimely deaths. Again, Vornholt writes that "13 of 20 people who were present at the opening of King Tut's burial chamber died within a few years." Vornholt does not give his source for this information, but it is clearly incorrect. The truth is that the newspapers at the time had a field day with the curse. Whenever anyone related to Carnarvon or the discovery of the tomb died, the death was taken as proof that the curse was in effect.

However, Egyptologist Herbert E. Winlock examined the evidence some 12 years after the tomb's opening. Of the 26 people present at the opening of the burial chamber, only 6 had died within the next 10 years. When King Tut's sarcophagus was opened, 22 of the 26 people were present, but only 2 of them had died within 10 years afterward. Finally, only 10 of the 26 people had watched the unwrapping of the mummy. *And none of them had died*

KING TUT'S CURSE ?

EVENT	NUMBER OF PEOPLE THERE	NUMBER OF DEATHS AFTER 10 YEARS
Burial chamber opening	26	6
Sarcophagus opening	22	2
Mummy unwrapping	10	0

within the next decade! In fact, many of the people who had the most contact with the king's mummy lived long and productive lives.

Perhaps the last word about the Carnarvon curse should belong to Sir Henry Rider Haggard, who wrote at the time that the idea of the curse was simply nonsense and "dangerous because it goes to swell the rising tide of superstition which at present seems to be overflowing the world."

MUMMY FINDER: The mummy of King Tutankhamen now rests in the Museum of Ancient Egyptian Art in Luxor, Egypt. According to author Nicholas Reeves, it has been placed in a box inside the outer coffin. Although visitors to the museum can look at the coffin, they cannot glimpse the king's mummy.

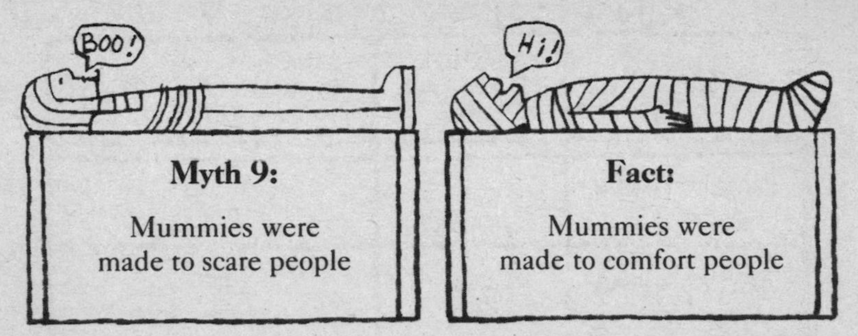

BOO!
Hi!
Myth 9:
Mummies were
made to scare people
Fact:
Mummies were
made to comfort people

This myth is related to Myth 8. Many people assume that mummies must be cursed because they are so scary. Nothing could be further from the truth. Egyptians mummified their dead to prepare them for an afterlife. To them, preserving the body after death was simply a way to conquer death.

Most people fear death, despite the fact that (as mummy researchers Aidan and Eve Cockburn wrote) "everything that lives must die." This is what is frightening — not the mummy itself. In fact, by mummifying an individual, Egyptians felt much better, since they believed they had continued the person's life.

According to the Cockburns, most people around the world

> believe in some form of life after death and often come to the conclusion that the body of the deceased should be prepared for this continuing existence. This can be achieved either by burying the person along with objects for use in the next life or, better still, by preserving the body itself. . . . [A]lmost all dead bodies in the United States today are embalmed. This can have no other purpose but to give survivors reassurance that life continues in some way: From the purely public health point of view, it is meaningless.

Some cultures also thought that mummifying the dead would stop their ghosts from returning to haunt the living. By making a dead person comfortable and happy, the living would be happier, too. If the thought of mummies scares you, try to picture yourself as a member of a civilization that practiced mummification, and take comfort.

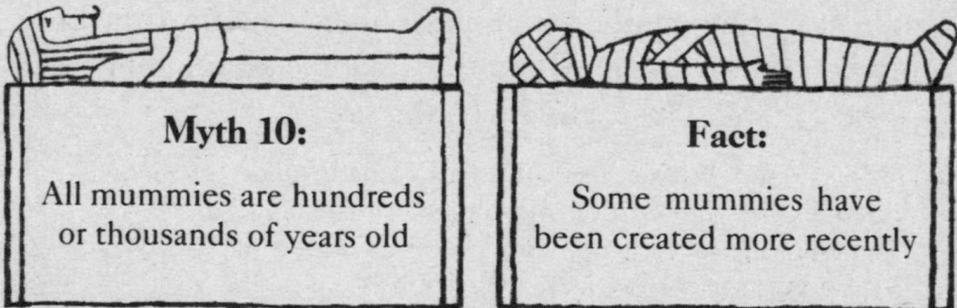

Myth 10:
All mummies are hundreds or thousands of years old
Fact:
Some mummies have been created more recently

Although most mummies were made intentionally or unintentionally many years ago, some mummies are more recent, and they are almost always accidental. For example, the mummified bodies of soldiers killed during

World Wars I and II have been found in various swamps in Europe.

In another example, Joseph Stalin, once the leader of the Soviet Union, was, according to many historians, responsible for the murder of millions of people during the Great Purge in the late 1930s. The secret police were ordered to arrest, question, and kill anyone suspected of being a counterrevolutionary. Numerous murders took place in Siberia, where the victims were quickly and quietly buried along the banks of the Ob River. Writer Adam Hochschild explains that many of the bodies became mummies because they were buried in dry, cold sand that lay on top of permanently frozen soil.

Then, in 1979, the bodies began to surface along the river. Although the secret police quickly built a wall and cordoned off the riverbank so that nearby townspeople wouldn't discover the crime, a sixty-two-year-old machinist and his mother were passengers on a boat traveling past the riverbank when they saw the secret police at work. He told Hochschild what he saw:

> The sun was setting. I saw this hastily made fence, and a lot of people. But the boat was blowing its whistle, and I didn't dare go ashore to investigate. Then the boat was on the move past the grave; the corpses were well lit by the sun.

Obviously, this accidental process was not intended by the murderers.

A recent discovery of an unintentional mummy occurred after the World Trade Center in New York City was bombed in February 1993. The body of one victim was missing for many weeks. Alfredo Mercado, who worked at a nearby hotel, had no reason to be at the site of the blast, but when investigators could not locate him, they concluded that he must have been killed in the parking garage beneath the tower. However, dogs trained to find corpses turned up no leads. Eventually, his body was recovered in the rubble beneath the bomb crater. Covered by a large slab of concrete, it had been mummified by the freezing weather. These facts explain why the dogs had not been able to detect his remains.

A very rare type of human mummy was discovered in Boise, Idaho, in early 1994, according to newspaper wire services. Neighbors of a man living in a condominium complex became concerned one day when he did not answer the doorbell.

They asked a retired doctor named Robert McKean to check on the man. To his surprise, the front door was unlocked, and Dr. McKean entered the apartment. He quickly discovered that the man was too sick to move.

Then Dr. McKean noticed the man's elderly mother lying on a couch in the back living room. She too could not move, but for a very different reason: she had been dead for seven years. For whatever reason, the man had not reported his mother's death and had continued to live with her as her body became mummified.

Accidental mummies aren't the only ones made today. For example, most medical students dissect a special type of human mummy — cadavers preserved in a solution of formaldehyde — to learn about anatomy. But officials at the Orange Coast College in Costa Mesa, California, had a better idea for mummifying the cadavers: first, the bodies were dehydrated, then injected and coated with silicone, a type of plastic. Next, the cadavers were cut into slices, so that sections could be removed and the internal organs viewed. This process doesn't smell, and plastic mummies can easily be reused, so fewer cadavers are needed.

But you may wish to make some personal mummy plans. For example, you can decide to have your pet mummified by a company in Salt Lake City. You can also sign yourself up to be mummified at death at Lynn

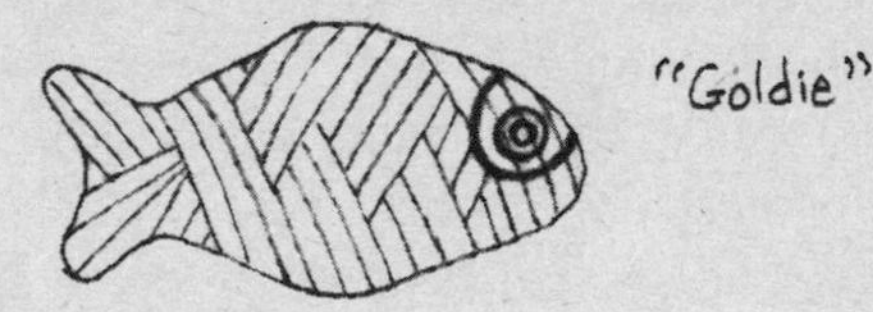

University in Boca Raton, Florida. Under the direction of John Cheu, a special program at the Institute of Funeral Services and Anatomy permits people to be mummified, using the best Egyptian techniques. So far, a number of people have registered for the program, but none have yet died.

No one knows if this is merely a fad or something that may have wider appeal. What do you think?

Now that you know the truth about mummies, you are ready to learn about the mummymaking process in more detail. The next two chapters will introduce you to intentional and accidental mummymaking.

3. The Art of Artificial Mummymaking

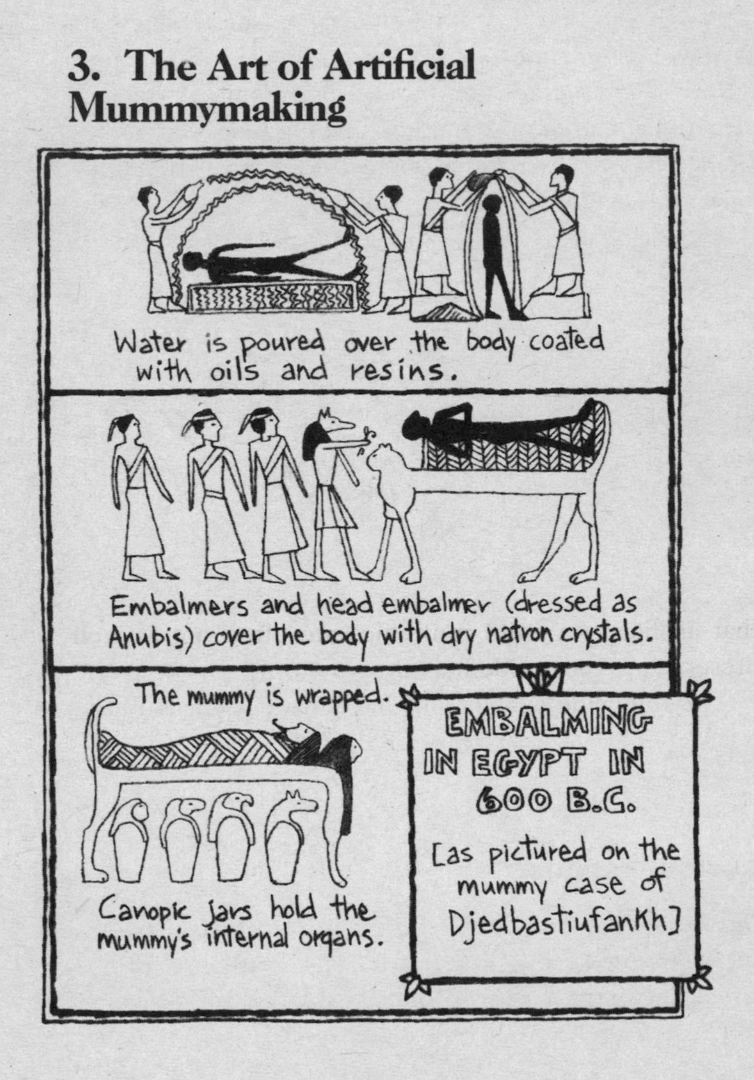

Water is poured over the body coated with oils and resins.
Embalmers and head embalmer (dressed as Anubis) cover the body with dry natron crystals.
The mummy is wrapped.
Canopic jars hold the mummy's internal organs.
EMBALMING IN EGYPT IN 600 B.C.
[as pictured on the mummy case of Djedbastiufankh]

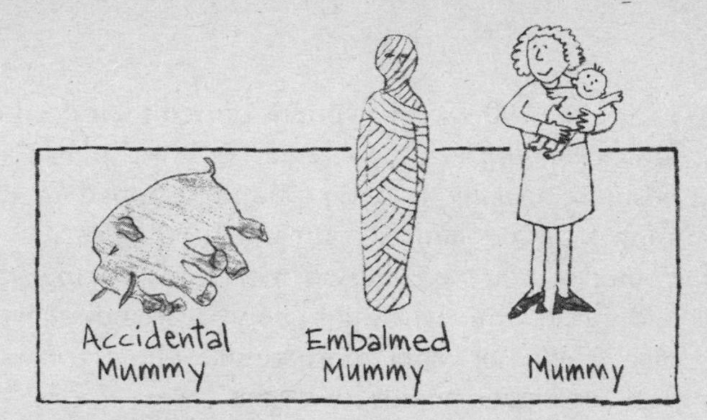

Some scientists who study mummies are quite fussy in their definition of the word. Two such men, Sir Grafton Elliot Smith and Warren R. Dawson, published a book on Egyptian mummies in 1924. In it, they wrote that *true* mummies are "bodies embalmed and preserved by artificial means." That is, only bodies that were deliberately treated by embalmers could be considered "mummies." They considered accidental mummies to be freaks of nature. Smith and Dawson admitted, however, that artificial (or true) mummies are often not as well preserved as the accidental ones.

The following civilizations have made artificial mummies:

Ancient Egyptian

Despite what many people think, ancient Egyptians did not at first make mummies artificially. Rather, they observed the natural process that took place after they buried their dead.

Before 3000 B.C., Egyptians buried their dead in shallow graves in the desert. The body was put in a flexed position, usually face down and wrapped in linen or animal skins, and accompanied with small objects. Poorer people were buried with knives or pots of food and water, while wealthier people were buried with jewelry, combs, or other adornments. The grave was lined with reed mats, boards, or bricks.

Then an amazing — and quite natural — thing happened. The hot sand that pressed up against the body quickly soaked the fluids from it and dried out the body's tissues before they could decay. When animal scavengers like the jackal (who might dig up a body in search of food) and human scavengers (who might rob graves of jewelry or other goods) uncovered the bodies, the Egyptians realized that the dead had been preserved.

Whether this helped form the Egyptians' religious beliefs or whether their views were developed before they understood how sand burial preserved bodies, no one knows. Nonetheless, mummification was an important part of ancient Egyptians' religion. Here's why:

The ancient Egyptians believed that inside the heart of every person was a spirit called *ka*. The ka resembled the living person in every way, but it was not released from the body until death. Egyptians would say, for example, that a woman "went to her ka," meaning that she had died. The ka lived an afterlife. But it could also die, they believed, unless a likeness of the person was placed in the burial chamber to become the ka's home. It was crucial, therefore, that the ka recognize the likeness, since no other shelter could keep it alive. Sometimes a small statue of the person was used; more often a mummy of the person was created. In order to stay alive, the ka also needed sustenance, which explains why food and water were placed in the chamber.

Some people may think that the Egyptians were obsessed with the idea of death; in truth, they loved life so much that they wanted it to continue in the next world. The fact that the dead were well preserved in the shallow graves was definitely comforting: the ka would be able to live.

Eventually, the idea of a sand burial did not appeal to members of the royal family and wealthy persons — they wanted something fancier. Between the years 3100 and

2686 B.C., some bodies were buried in coffins that were placed in underground tombs. However, the coffins and the large empty chambers eliminated the ingredients necessary for accidental mummification. Since hot sand no longer surrounded the body, it could not soak up the body's fluids. And in the damp burial chambers, the bodies began to rot.

That led to the need to make mummies artificially. In trying to copy the work done by the sand and sun, ancient Egyptians employed a number of mummymaking methods.

Molded mummies. From 2686–2181 B.C., Egyptian mummymakers experimented with "stucco mummies." They draped bodies with linen, covered them with plaster, and attempted to mold the body and facial features to keep them as natural-looking as possible, like a statue.

Professor H. Junker, writing in the *Journal of Egyptian Archaeology*, described two stucco mummies he uncovered around 1913:

> In two graves we found the [bodies] covered with a layer of stucco-plaster, a method of treatment which is entirely peculiar. First of all the corpse was covered with a fine linen cloth, with the special purpose of preventing the mass of plaster from getting into the mouth, ears, nose, and so on. Then the plaster was put on and modelled according to the form of the body, the head being in one case so accurately followed that one can clearly see the fallen-in nose and twisted mouth.

Another stucco mummy — discovered at Saqqâra, Egypt, in 1966 — is so well preserved, according to

Egyptologist A. J. Spencer, that the face is virtually lifelike, down to its wig, mustache, and false beard. Another writer, Carol Andrews, points out that an observer can easily spot a callus on the bottom of one foot. No matter how real stucco mummies appeared, however, their insides usually decayed, leaving only a skeleton.

In an improvement on the stucco technique, linen bandages soaked in resin were used to wrap and stuff the mummy to preserve the features. Smith and Dawson described one mummy of this type on display at the museum of the Royal College of Surgeons in London. The embalmers, they wrote, molded

> the mass carefully into shape, bestowing the minutest care to every detail of the form of the body. The details of the face, which is now somewhat distorted owing to the wrinkling of the linen and to the breakage of the nose in ancient times, are emphasized by paint, the eyes, eyebrows, and moustache being carefully traced. . . . The body cavity is closely packed with resin-soaked linen. The head (which has been broken from the trunk) rattles when shaken. Some free matter is therefore within the skull.

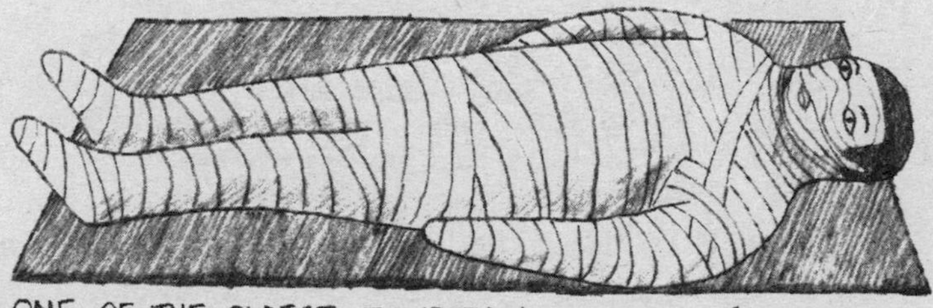

ONE OF THE OLDEST EGYPTIAN MUMMIES (2400 B.C.)

The best mummies. By the Twenty-first Dynasty (from about 1090–945 B.C.), mummymakers in Egypt had hit upon two important components of successful preservation — the removal of the internal organs, and the drying out of the body with a saltlike substance called natron. Depending on how much money a person could pay, the mummymaking process differed dramatically. The Greek historian Herodotus described the most expensive technique, the medium-priced technique, and the least expensive technique.

Of the most expensive technique, he wrote:

> First they draw out the brains through the nostrils with an iron hook, taking part of it out in this manner, the rest by infusion of drugs. Then with a sharp Ethiopian stone they make an incision in the side, and take out all the [internal organs]; and having cleansed the abdomen and rinsed it with palm-wine, they next sprinkle it with pounded perfumes. Then having filled the belly with pure myrrh . . . and cassia, and other perfumes . . . they sew it up again; and when they have done this, they steep it in [natron], leaving it under for 70 days. . . . At the end of the 70 days they wash the corpse and wrap the whole body in bandages of flaxen cloth, smearing it with gum, which the Egyptians commonly use instead of glue.

brain hooks

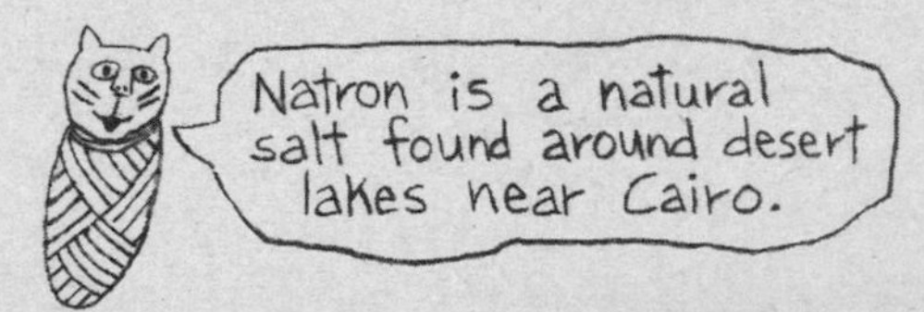

Natron is a natural salt found around desert lakes near Cairo.

Afterward, they placed the body in a coffin shaped like a man or woman and set it, upright, in a burial tomb.

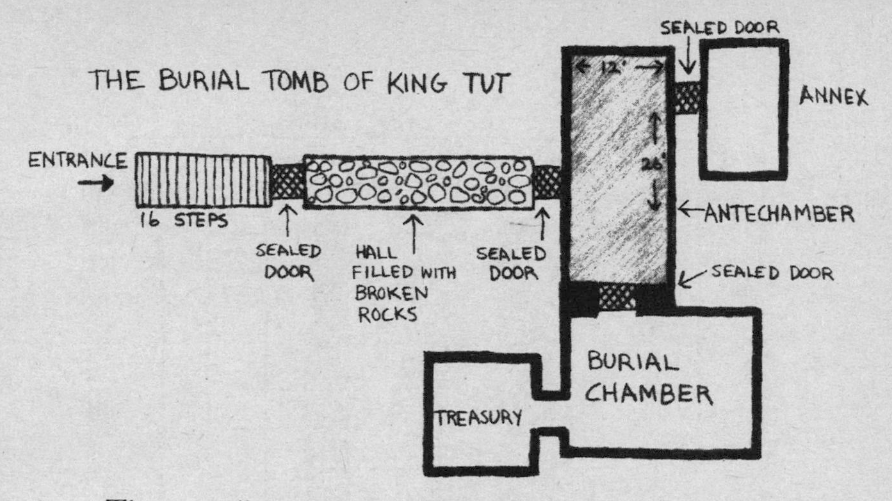

The medium-priced mummification, Herodotus noted, omitted the removal of the internal organs. Instead, the body was filled with a natron solution, which helped dissolve the internal organs. After a time, they flushed the natron from the body.

As for the least expensive method, the body was merely soaked in salt and hot bitumen (a tarlike substance) or salt alone. Most Egyptologists agree that bodies treated with salt and bitumen were the first to be called mummies, since the word *mummy*, it is thought, comes from the word for bitumen in Arabic.

During this period, embalmers sometimes added one other important technique to make the mummy look more lifelike: they padded the face and body with various materials, such as sawdust, mud, cloth, or even butter. Because the eyeballs quickly deteriorated, artificial eyes made of stone or cloth were also used.

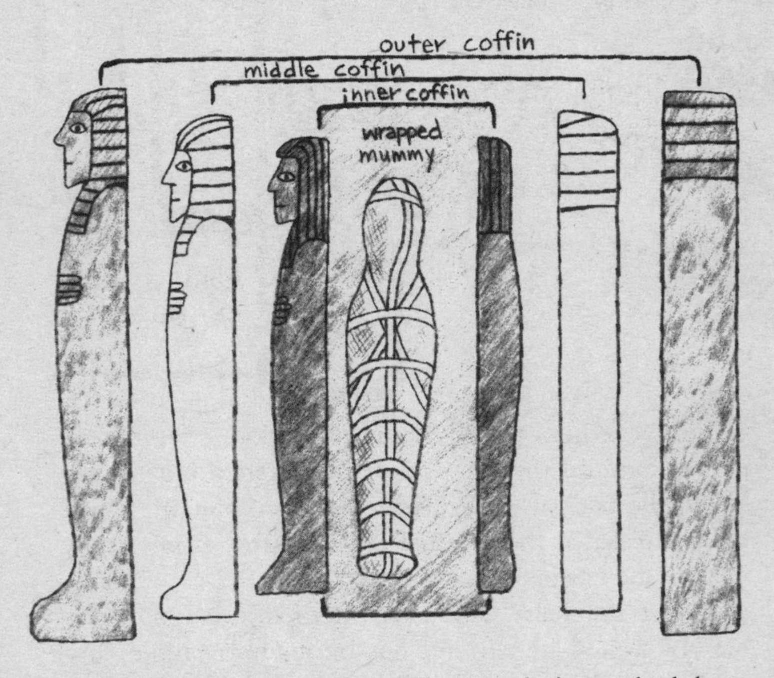

By 600 B.C., these excellent techniques had been gradually abandoned, and more emphasis was placed on the outward appearance of the mummy rather than the preservation of the body. After Egypt was conquered by the Greeks in 305 B.C., the appearance of the coffin became as important as that of the mummy. The coffin sometimes bore a portrait of the person, painted on wood during his or her life. Inside, the mummy would be decoratively wrapped in linen, often in a geometric pattern. Underneath the wrappings, however, the body was poorly preserved.

Andes

Although Egyptian mummies are the first that come to most people's minds, artificial mummification was practiced first by ancestors of the Incan empire who lived in and around the Andes Mountains of South America. There were many different civilizations within the Andes range, and they did not use one method of mummymaking. But, like the Egyptians, they all shared a belief in the importance of the afterlife. According to archaeologist Brian Fagan, bodies of the dead were treated the same way as holy objects.

Chinchoros mummies. Near the border of present-day Peru and Chile along the Pacific coast, the Chinchoros civilization was once found. Archaeologist Michael E. Moseley says that the Chinchoros were the first people in the world to practice mummification. They preserved their dead beginning about 5000 B.C., reaching a peak in 3000 B.C., around the same time that the Egyptians began experimenting with mummification.

The methods used by the Chinchoros were quite different from those of the Egyptians. The Chinchoros literally took the dead person's body apart, treated it, and reassembled it. As the body was put back together, morticians strengthened the limbs and spinal column by inserting sticks under the skin. They packed the body with various materials, including clay and feathers. Finally, the mummy was covered with a coat of clay. The face

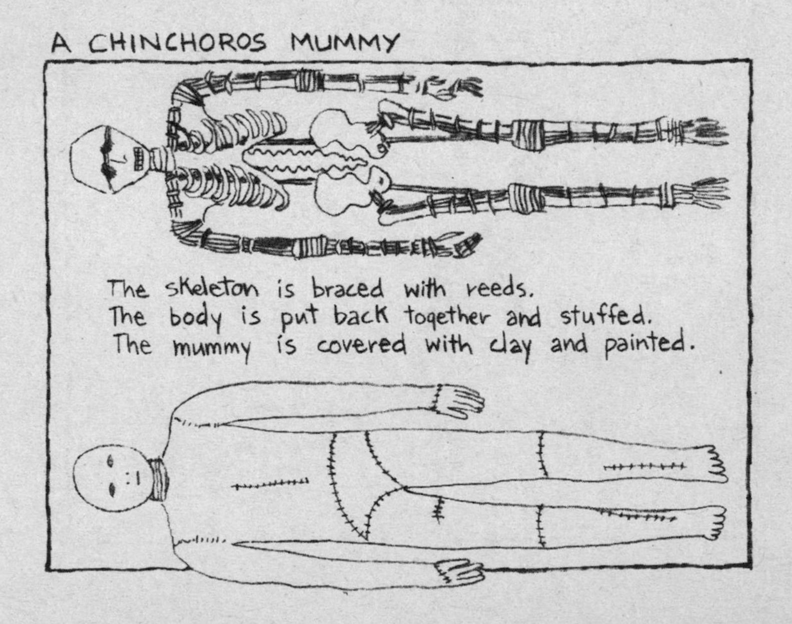
A CHINCHOROS MUMMY
The skeleton is braced with reeds.
The body is put back together and stuffed.
The mummy is covered with clay and painted.

was painted with features, and a wig was attached. Many such mummies have been recovered. The face of one Chinchoros mummy had been painted many times, leading some archaeologists to suggest that the mummy had been displayed for a long time before it was finally buried.

Paracas mummies. Around 400 B.C., mummification was also practiced in the fishing village of Paracas, according to Moseley. However, not all archaeologists agree that these mummies were intentionally made. In Paracas, bodies were put into "mummy bundles" before they were placed in a large underground necropolis, or

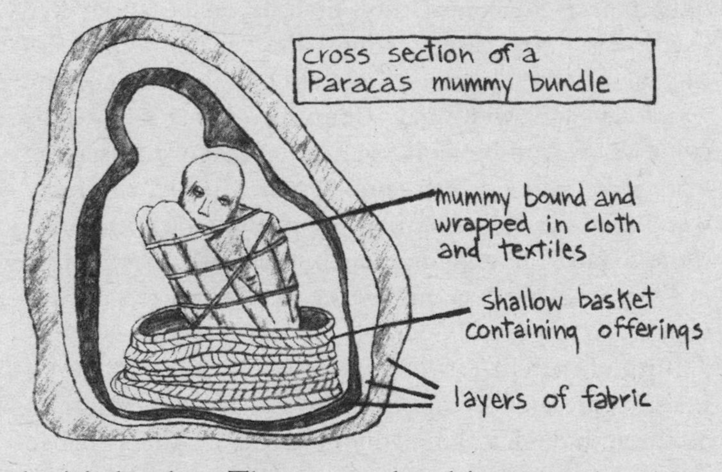

burial chamber. They were placed in a seated position and bound tightly with cord. Then they were covered with cotton cloth and wrapped with brightly decorated fabric. Archaeologists conclude that when the person was

important in the community, more layers of fabric were used. In one case, writes the author Georgess McHargue, the cloth used to wrap one Paracas mummy was four yards wide and twenty-two yards long. This cloth was woven by hand, so a great deal of painstaking work was involved in its production. Finally, the body was placed in a coiled basket and taken to the necropolis. More than 429 human mummy bundles have been found in Paracas, as well as bundles containing parrots, foxes, dogs, cats, frogs, and deer.

But did the citizens of Paracas intend to make mummies? Some archaeologists believe that mummification occurred through a natural drying process. Others believe that resins were used to prepare the bodies. But until further studies take place and the results are compared, no one will know for certain.

Incan royal mummies. From A.D. 1438–1532 — well after the Chinchoros and Paracas civilizations became part of the Incan empire — Incan kings and family members were mummified artificially. Anthropologist James Vreeland notes that when a king died, his body was seated on a special throne. His arms were crossed over his chest, his knees were drawn up to his chest, and his head was bent down over his knees. Pieces of silver or gold were put into the king's fists or mouth. Finally, his body was dressed in fancy cloth and wrapped in cotton fabric and his face was covered.

Exactly how the kings were mummified is a mystery. However it was done, a month after the death, the king was placed in a sepulcher along with his used clothing, fingernail and toenail clippings, and any hair that had been cut from his head during his lifetime. A few of his favorite wives, his servants, and llamas were sacrificed, mummified, and buried with the king. Then the king's body was removed from the sepulcher, given to his surviving family, and cared for by special attendants, who, Vreeland wrote,

> carried out routine chores such as whisking the flies from the mummy's brow, changing and washing its clothing, [and] calling in visitors with whom the Incan wished to "speak."

The king's mummy would attend religious and rainmaking ceremonies and sometimes visit other royal mummies. According to writer Bernabé Cobo, the attendants

> sat [the royal mummies] down in the plaza in a row, in order of seniority, and the servants who looked after them ate and drank there. . . . The dead toasted one another, and they drank to the living and vice versa.

On special occasions members of the general public were allowed to see the mummified kings.

After the Spanish conquest of the Inca, Garcilaso de la Vega described his encounter in 1559 with a number of royal Incan mummies, including the famous ruler Huayna Capac:

> The bodies were so intact that they lacked neither hair, eyebrows nor eyelashes. They were in clothes just as they had worn when alive, with *llautus* [headbands] . . . but no other signs of royalty. They were seated in the way Indian men and women usually sit, and their eyes were cast down. . . . I remember touching the finger of Huayna Capac. It was hard

The mummy of an Incan ruler is carried in a parade during the Incan Festival of the Dead.

From a drawing from the early 1600s

> and rigid, like that of a wooden statue. The bodies weighed so little that any Indian could carry them from house to house in his arms or on his shoulders. They carried them wrapped in white shrouds through the streets and plazas, the Indians dropping to their knees, making reverences with groans and tears, and many Spaniards removing their caps.

In general, the Spaniards were disturbed by the ancestor worship that seemed to accompany the Incan mummies. Eventually, the conqueror Pizarro ordered the burning of all royal mummies.

Incan sacrificial mummies. High in the Andes Mountains that surrounded the core of the Incan empire, many humans were sacrificed and, because of the altitude, quickly mummified. These were often young boys, who may have been the sons of nobility. Juan Schobinger, who has studied these mummies, believes they were sacrificed for two reasons: to show that the Inca were in charge of the mountains and to make offerings to the sun god.

The mummy of an eight- or nine-year-old boy, dating from Incan times, was found near the top of Cerro El Plomo, a 17,815-foot mountain in Chile. Author Thomas Besom writes that the boy's face

> was painted red, with four yellow lines on each side radiating from his nose and upper lip to his cheeks. . . . His long, black hair was oiled and plaited into more than 200 tiny braids. On his head he wore a band made of human hair and a headdress of black llama hair decorated with condor feathers.

Despite the altitude, he was wearing only a sleeveless wool tunic and cloak as well as moccasins made from

llama skin. His body was adorned with jewelry, including a pendant shaped like a sideways H and a wide silver bracelet on his right arm. Near him was a bag of coca leaves and five small pouches filled with his baby hair, baby teeth, and fingernail clippings. At that time and place it was customary to save such items and place them in pouches near the dead person, so that, according to Besom, "his spirit would not have to search for" the items after death.

How was the boy killed? Scientists found frostbite on his fingers and swollen ankles and feet. This suggests that he had walked a long way before he reached the top of the mountain and was alive long enough for frostbite to set in. Once he was near the intended sacrificial spot, he was probably given some beer to intoxicate him; then the people who had accompanied him to the mountain left him there. Tired from the long hike and drowsy from the beer, he crouched down to keep warm. He probably fell asleep and froze to death. Some five hundred years later, his body was found.

MUMMY FINDER: Today, the boy is on display in Chile's National Museum of Natural History in Santiago.

Scythian

The Scythians, a people made up of many tribes who lived in southern Russia from the eighth to the fourth century B.C., also mummified their dead kings. The Greek writer Herodotus visited the Scythians and described what they did when a king died. After digging a large, square grave,

> they take the king's corpse and having opened the belly, and cleaned out the inside, fill the cavity with a preparation of chopped cypress, frankincense, parsley-seed, and anise-seed, after which they sew up the opening, enclose the body in wax, and placing it on a wagon, carry it about through all the different tribes.

On seeing the body, every man in the tribe had to sever a piece of his ear, cut his hair short, make a cut all the way around his arm, make a hole in his forehead and nose, and finally, as if this weren't enough, drive an arrow completely through his left hand.

After the king's body was shown to each tribe, it was taken to Gerrhi, the most remote area of the Scythian territory, and buried. At that time, his servants were killed, usually by strangulation. Then earth was thrown into the grave and a tall mound was built.

But the most important part of the ceremony took place a year later. Fifty of the dead king's best attendants were strangled along with fifty of the king's most beautiful horses. Then their internal organs were removed and their abdomens were filled with chaff and sewn shut.

Scythian horseman as pictured on a tapestry buried with a chief

Next the Scythians dug a large circular grave around the king's burial mound. Each horse was placed in the grave, staked down so that it looked as if it were galloping. Onto each horse a strangled and mummified attendant was placed — with a large stake driven down the spinal cord and through the horse. Then all were covered with earth — a ring of mummified horses with mummified riders encircling the grave of the beloved king.

MUMMY FINDER: Few Scythian mummies exist today, but some (men and horses) are on display at the Hermitage Museum in St. Petersburg, Russia.

South Sea

Many mummies from Australia, Papua New Guinea, and islands in the Torres Strait have been found, according to the anthropologists Graeme Pretty and Angela Calder.

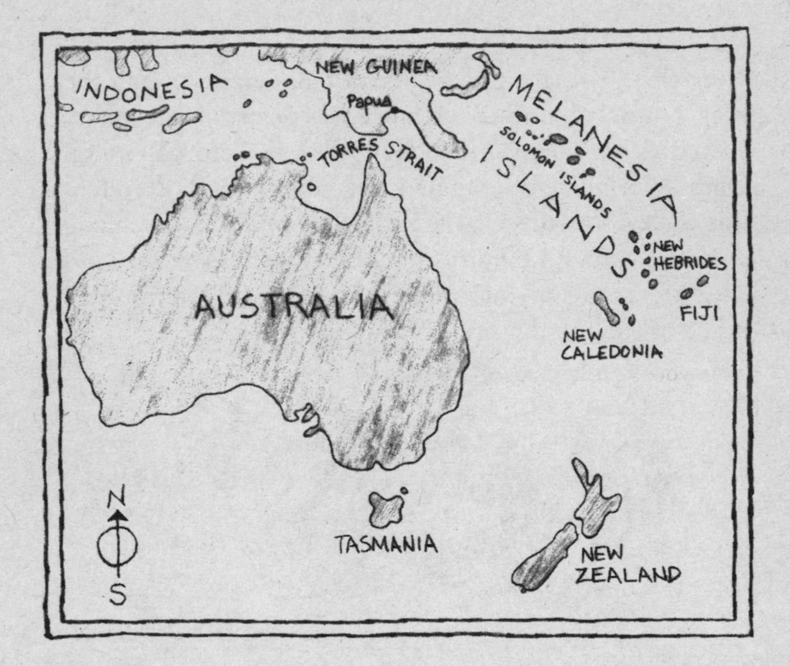

In Australia, some aboriginal tribes tied a corpse into a sitting position and left it outdoors until dried by the sun. Then, instead of burial, they placed the body in the branches of a tree or on a raised wooden platform.

Some tribes helped speed the mummification process by sewing the mouth, eyes, and other orifices closed and then smoking the body in order to dry it. Before doing this, they took out all the fat from the body, mixed it with red ocher, and smeared it on the skin. Then, write Pretty and Calder, fires were

> kindled underneath the platform, and the friends and mourners take up their position around it, where they remain about 10 days, during the whole of which time the mourners are not allowed to speak; a guard is placed on each side of the corpse, whose duty it is to keep off the flies with bunches of emu feathers or small branches of trees. . . . After the body has remained several weeks on the platform, it is taken down and buried [in a tree or on another platform]; the skull becomes the drinking cup of the nearest relation. Bodies thus preserved have the appearance of mummies; there is no sign of decay; and the wild dogs will not meddle with them, though they devour all manner of carrion.

In a somewhat different version, people from Melanesia, the islands north of Australia, allowed the body to sit out for a few days before they put it (by then quite swollen) into a canoe and sailed it away from land. Its skin was peeled off and the internal organs were removed and replaced with palm pith; the brain was also removed. Finally, the body was taken back to shore, tied to a wooden frame, and hung to dry. In order to make sure that it dried properly, small holes were made in the knees, elbows, hands, and feet to help bodily fluids drain. At this time, the tongue, the palms of the hands, and the soles of the feet were removed and given to the surviving spouse.

After a number of months, when the mummy was dried, it was decorated with seashell eyes, grass, and seeds, and was painted in red ocher. The mummy was then tied to the center post of the home of its spouse. As Pretty and Calder note, "when, in the course of time, it fell to pieces, the head only was retained."

If these practices seem somewhat gruesome, Pretty and Calder remind the reader that there were reasons for such methods. In Melanesia, for example, the grieving family used mummification as a way of making sure that the dead person would be present for a longer period of time. If they could stop the body from decomposing, they would have the company of the relative longer.

A number of other civilizations also practiced artificial mummymaking. You'll read about one (the Guanches) later. For now, though, it's time to learn how mummies were created by accident.

Part of a Scythian tattoo

4. Mummies by Accident

In ways that sometimes seem quite mysterious, atmospheric and environmental conditions work together to create accidental mummies. These are usually found in extreme climates: the hottest (and driest) climates as well as the coldest (and driest) climates. But don't jump to the conclusion that mummies and water don't mix, because other mummies have been found in the remnants of swamps and bogs.

Here are three ways that mummies have been accidentally produced.

Method 1: Desiccation

Some mummies have been created through the process known as desiccation. This happens when dry soil or air comes into contact with a dead body, thus preserving it.

One of the best places to dry out a mummy, other than in hot desert sand, is in a cave. Perhaps as many as two hundred mummies who were ancestors of present-day southwestern Native Americans have been found. Many of these mummies are incomplete (sometimes only a limb remains, rather than a complete body) and most were buried sometime between A.D. 100 and A.D. 1300.

Ventana Cave, located on the Papago reservation in Arizona, was studied in the 1940s by noted anthropologist Emil W. Haury. The cave is in a desert area of Arizona that receives only about seven or eight inches of rain a year. The soil is extremely dry, and no crops can be cultivated unless the land is irrigated. The area also lacks high humidity. These three factors — high temperatures, dry soil, and low humidity — helped produce a natural mummification process for Native Americans buried in local caves.

The Papago Indians permitted Haury to study and excavate the cave. He was particularly interested in it because he had seen human bones on the cave's floor. In fact, as Haury wrote in his book *The Stratigraphy and Archaeology of Ventana Cave,* some mummies "were practically at surface level, the toes and sandals of one (Number 9) having been scorched by a Papago fire."

The Papago and their ancestors have used Ventana Cave for many centuries, both as a shelter and as a source of spring water. To them, the cave has two names: *Chiu*

Vafia, or Spring Cave, and *Hewultki*, or Whirlwind House. Both names are particularly appropriate for the cave, according to Haury.

The Papago believed that once the wind lived in the cave and took a dislike to any fires built there except those that used mesquite wood. What's more, there was a spot in the cave near the spring where it was dangerous to build any fire. If a fire was started there, a whirlwind would whip up and "blow your head off." Even Haury's helpers found this tale to be true:

> Two of our workmen camped in the cave in 1934 during a rainy spell and, forgetting [the whirlwind spot], built a fire of ironwood in the forbidden spot. The result of this transgression was as if "dynamite had been put in the fire." Coals were blown all over the cave, their blankets were burned and they had to run out in the rain.

When Haury and his workers began to excavate the cave in 1941, they discovered thirty-nine bodies (though not all were complete). All of the remains were judged to have been buried between the years A.D. 1000 and A.D. 1400. During the course of those four hundred years, different groups of people buried some of their dead in the cave. They chose to place them away from the spring, perhaps aware that it could become contaminated. They also continued to use the cave for shelter, which led Haury to conclude that they "held no fear of the dead."

About twenty-five of the bodies were adults. A shallow

grave was dug and the bodies were placed in the earth. Sometimes the bodies were flexed; other times they were extended. More attention was paid to the graves of the infants and children. Some were grass-lined, or the bodies were covered with grass. Many people were buried with objects, such as pottery bowls, placed over their heads. Sometimes a pillow was put under the head.

The dry soil and the climate of the cave combined to turn ten of the burials into mummies. One well-preserved mummy was probably an important member of the community, judging by the number of items found

with him. He wore shell earrings attached through the earlobes with cotton string. He also wore a nose plug and had a yucca cord that may have held a pendant around his neck. With him were a quiver, arrows, and a "work kit," as Haury called it. Among other things, the kit contained awls made from bone, a cactus-spine needle, cloth fragments, cord made from human hair, a human-hair wig, and small pieces of stitched sandals. Haury believed that the man clearly valued cloth and probably sewed.

As for the man's place in his community, Haury wrote that

> no other burials were equipped with so many tangible goods, no others were wearing nose plugs or jewelry. The wigs and charms may mean that he was endowed with special powers. Perhaps he was . . . a respected old gentleman.

Although bodies can be mummified by placing them in dry soil, the same process can occur in the protected environment of warm caves. Many mummified bodies have been found in dry, warm volcanic caves of the Aleutian Islands of Alaska. About fifty years ago, according to author Don Brothwell, quite a number of them were taken to the Smithsonian Institution in Washington, D.C., for analysis. There, archaeologists and anthropologists discovered that the internal organs had been removed, and grass stuffed in their place. Finally, the body was put in a flexed position and tied. Some scientists also think that the Aleut may have smoked the bodies to help the mummification process.

Method 2: Freezing

Freezing is a fast way to make an accidental mummy, and many mummies have been produced in dry, frigid climates. One remarkable discovery was recorded by Jens Peder Hart Hansen in *The Greenland Mummies*.

On October 9, 1972, Hans Grønvold and his brother Jokum were hunting near the former coastal settlement of Qilakitsoq, Greenland. This is a desolate area; the small settlement there was most likely abandoned sometime in the 1400s. Hans Grønvold was surprised to find two bodies lying under a rock. As he wrote in a letter to a friend:

> I found the grave while hunting for ptarmigan along a route which I've always taken. I usually go past the foot of a cliff where the ground is flat and easy to walk on. That's when I noticed that the stone was irregular and the fallen stones were flat. Without thinking, I picked up a large stone. And then I saw a corpse, covered by a skin, which seemed to be fresh. I started to poke around and realized that I had found a grave which had never been opened before. . . . There was a half-grown child lying on top, close to what was probably its mother, and then we saw a doll which had fallen to the side, a doll which turned out to be a little child. We put them back in place, with the child to the very back, by the rock. Only the eyes and the mouth of the child were damaged, everything was dried up.

The Grønvolds later discovered that the grave actually contained two children and three women. Moments later, the two men found another grave containing the mummified bodies of three more women.

Although the discovery was interesting, none of the local authorities — nor anyone at the Greenland State Museum — wanted to investigate it further. Finally, in 1977, someone at the museum realized that a great deal of information could be obtained by examining the bodies. After the graves were dated to A.D. 1475, which made the mummies the oldest preserved remains in Greenland, researchers realized they had a special opportunity to study a part of Greenland's history. They chose to do so as nondestructively as possible.

The mummies of the younger child and three of the women were well preserved, and they were studied as found. Researchers did not undress them or even cut into them, except for a small incision made in the women's backs. The four other mummies were not particularly well preserved; their clothing was removed so that it and their bodies could be studied more carefully. This is what the researchers found:

Tattooing. Although the natural mummification process had turned the women's skin very dark, infrared photographs showed that five of the six women had been tattooed, as was customary with the Inuit. The photographs revealed that the tattooed women had black or

TATTOOED INUIT WOMEN MUMMIES

dark blue lines on their faces. The lines were on the forehead and arched over the eyebrows. Two of the women also had a dot tattooed onto their forehead. Each woman had tattooed cheeks, while three had lines tattooed beneath their chins.

Causes of death. The fact that the two graves contained women and children but no men puzzled researchers. They knew that the Inuit did not bury women and children separately from men. So they wondered if the eight had drowned together, perhaps when a boat capsized.

The evidence seemed to rule out this possibility. First, the body of a drowning victim would likely have many traces of minerals on it, and none of the women or children did. Second, they had not been buried according to Inuit custom. "The custom of our forefathers was to cover the drowned with the skin of the boat, because boats, kayaks, and tools linked to death could not be used again," one Inuit explained. "Our ancestors believed that if you used the implements of the dead, you too would meet misfortune."

Researchers tried to analyze the contents of the stomachs and intestines to determine if the people had died at the same time. If all had died during the same season, this might help prove that they had died together. As it turned out, only one mummy had any food in its intestines. This indicated that the woman had died during the summer, but researchers could find no evidence relating to when the other seven people had died.

Finally, the researchers were able to identify with some certainty the cause of death of only three people.

• One woman had a malignant tumor near the base of her skull which most likely caused her death.

• The older child had Calvé-Perthes disease, which afflicts the hip joint and which would have made him vulnerable to other life-threatening diseases. The authors of *The Greenland Mummies* write that the youngster

> must have badly needed support, being able only to limp or perhaps just crawl about. . . . Surprisingly, the soles of the boy's boots were heavily worn, repaired in fact, which seems contradictory to his condition.

However, the researchers suggested that, after his death, his boots were removed and another pair of boots was put on him. This seems to be a safe assumption, since the left and right boots had been put on the wrong feet. Although they could not pinpoint a precise cause of death, Calvé-Perthes disease would have been a factor.

• The younger child, a boy about six months old at death, appeared to have been buried alive. Because they did not want to destroy the mummy or its clothing, the researchers were limited to taking x-rays of the child.

These did not turn up any injuries or diseases. Had his mother died shortly before he was buried? Inuit custom at that time dictated that the child be buried alive or suffocated by its father if a woman could not be found to nurse it. Although such a practice seems cruel now, the Inuit believed that the child and its mother would travel to the land of the dead together. The researchers concluded that the child had been buried alive.

MUMMY FINDER: The six-month-old child and three of the female mummies are on permanent display at the Greenland National Museum in Nuuk.

Method 3: Absence of Air

Perhaps the most interesting type of accidental mummy is the bog body. These bodies — of people and animals — have been discovered in peat bogs primarily in northern Europe. In fact, more than 1,500 such bodies have been found in the last three or four hundred years, though most have not been preserved. Only a few are on display in museums in Denmark, England, Germany, and the Netherlands.

Bodies ended up in bogs in a number of ways. Some

people died there accidentally. After all, a bog is a dangerous place. An unsuspecting person who steps into a pool of bog water can become trapped in its spongy bottom layer, pulled in, and eventually drowned. Other people were killed and buried in the remote and unpopulated bogs or went there to commit suicide. Finally, even when a person died elsewhere, his body may have been buried in a bog for fear that he might become a ghost. Better that the person should haunt the bog than the town where he or she died!

Of course, it seems illogical that a person buried in a wet bog could turn into a mummy. But it did occur when three conditions were met. First, the water had to be deep enough to protect the body from attack by animals and insects. Second, the water had to be oxygen-free (that is, stagnant), so that no bacteria could live there, and contain tannic acid (used to turn hide into leather), so that the outer skin of the body began to tan. Finally, the water temperature had to be cold enough (normal refrigerator temperature, write authors Bryony

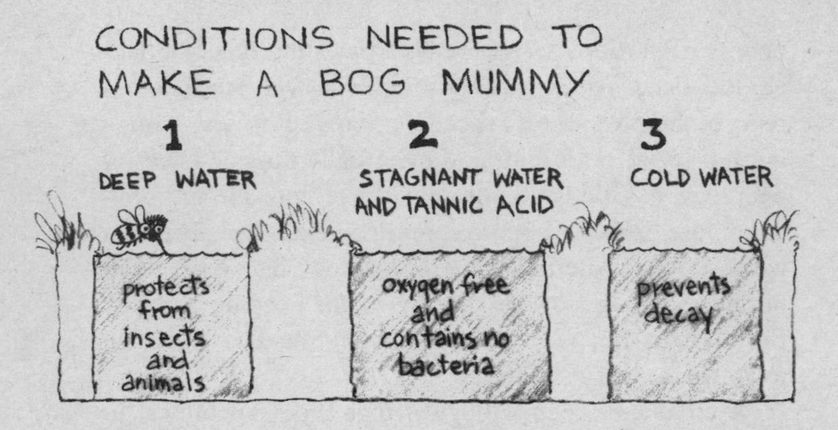

and John Coles) so that the body would not rot or decay. In short, a body can turn into a mummy when it is buried in a bog in deep water in winter.

Some say the most famous bog body ever found was a man in Tollund Mose, Denmark, in 1950. Because of the bog's location, he was called Tollund Man. Workers uncovered him as they cut blocks of peat. In fact, the body was still in peat when it was sent to the National Museum of Denmark for scientific analysis.

Buried about 2,000 years before, Tollund Man was between thirty and forty years old and wore only a leather cap and belt. The most striking feature is his head. It was in such excellent condition that the stubble on his chin was visible. He had a peaceful look on his face, his eyes closed, as if he were sleeping. But scientists quickly noted that he had been hanged, for a noose of braided leather had cut into his neck.

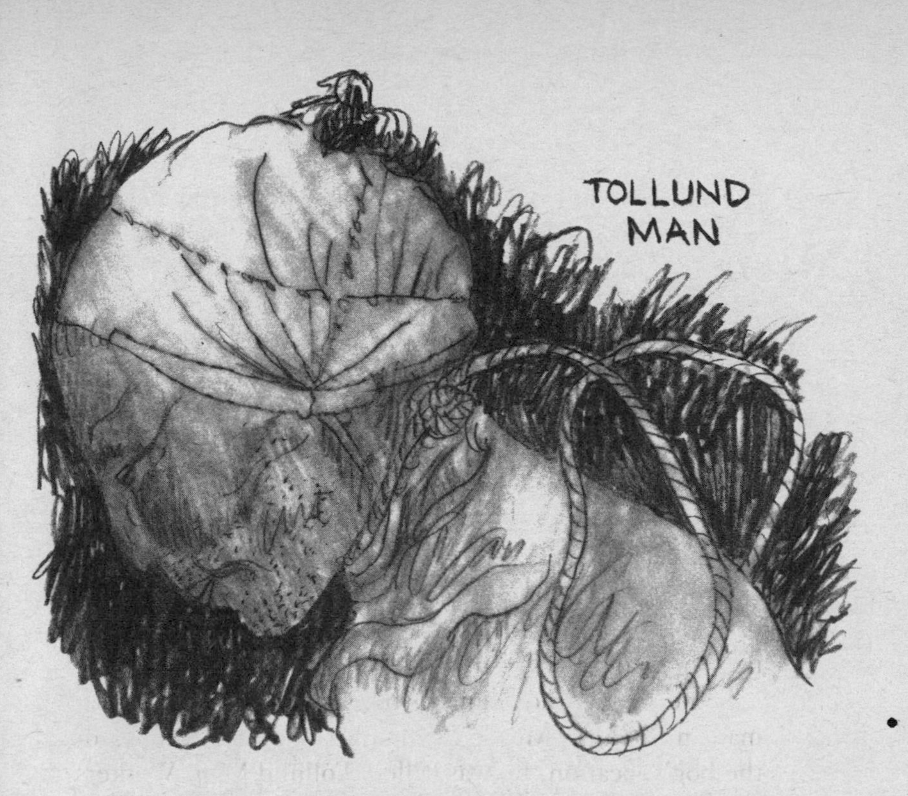

With the tools of modern science, researchers were able to determine what he had eaten during the last day of his life. They analyzed the contents of his stomach and found the remains of porridge, which was made of barley, linseed, willow herb seed, and about thirty other types of wild seeds. They concluded that he died in late winter or early spring, when only seeds and grains would be available for food.

Researchers were curious as to why Tollund Man was killed. They reason that if he had been a criminal, he would not have been found in a sleeping position. They also believe that his eyes and mouth were closed *after* he died. If this is true, it may mean he was sacrificed to the gods.

In the Iron Age, the man and his friends would have cut peat from the bog in Tollund. After a successful time of harvesting peat, perhaps Tollund Man was killed as an act of thanksgiving. Scientists think this may be so, for many other bog bodies have been found in bogs where peat was cut.

MUMMY FINDER: Tollund Man can be seen at the Silkeborg Museum in Silkeborg, Denmark.

Of course, even ideal peat bog conditions do not always safeguard a bog body once it is found. Here's what J. Wentworth Day wrote in describing a body found in Burwell Fen sometime between 1960 and 1971:

> Most shudderingly entrancing of all was the Ancient Briton, who suddenly emerged from the peat in Burwell Fen when the turf-diggers were at work. He stood upright in his dug-out canoe. His lank black hair dropped to his shoulders. The peat-dark skin was still stretched over the bones of his face. The eyes had gone but the eyesockets were dark with mystery. He was clad in a long leather jacket, belted, with garters round his legs and the right arm was raised as though about to cast a spear. That body of the unknown hunter, the nameless warrior, had been preserved in the peat for uncounted aeons of time. It crumbled to dust in the sharp Fen air.

Now that you know the facts about mummymaking, you're ready to learn exactly how scientists have succeeded in making mummies talk.

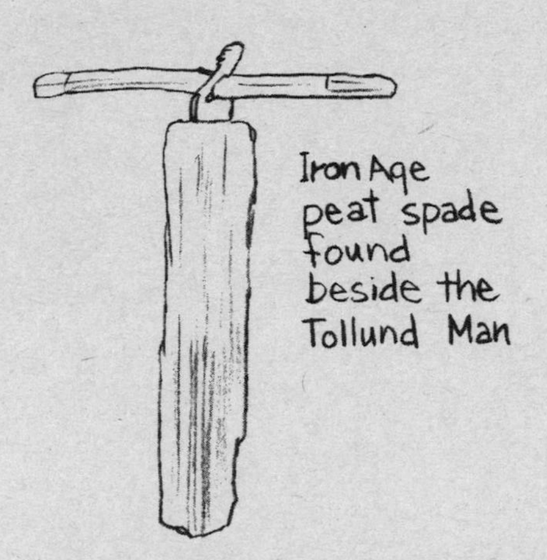

Iron Age
peat spade
found
beside the
Tollund Man

Part II
How to Make a Mummy Talk

5. How to Make a Mummy Talk

In order to study a mummy, scientists perform a number of procedures, similar in some ways to those used by a medical examiner who conducts an autopsy. Of course, it wasn't always like this. During the 1800s and early 1900s, when studying Egyptian mummies was a popular pastime, a mummy would be unrolled and destroyed in front of a number of invited guests. After the unwrapping was over, the mummy and its wrappings were simply thrown away. Today, scientists try to preserve the mummy under analysis. Because of this care and concern, people might think that mummies cannot provide as much information as they used to. However, thanks to the crusading work of many scientists, including Dr. A. Rosalie David of the Manchester Museum, most mummies studied with nondestructive methods not only survive such examination in good shape, they reveal much more information than in the past.

What exactly do scientists do, then? Here's a list of the steps a team will take to coax a mummy to talk and yet keep it safe:

Document its appearance with photographs. Before work on a mummy — especially an accidental one that was just discovered — is begun, a series of photographs will be taken to record every aspect of its appearance. In this way, scientists will be able to see if the mummy's condition starts to deteriorate or otherwise change.

X-ray the body completely. X-rays will reveal what is inside a wrapped mummy and the condition of the body.

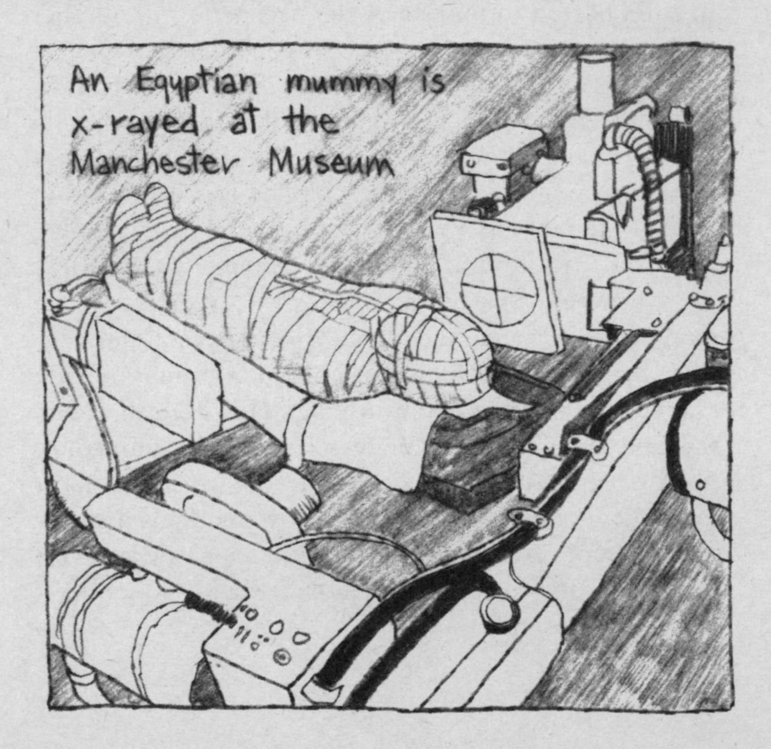
An Egyptian mummy is x-rayed at the Manchester Museum

Sometimes more than one body has been found inside a wrapped mummy; other times an extra head or leg or even a baby has been discovered. X-rays may also reveal certain diseases or afflictions that the person suffered. By using x-rays, a scientist does not have to unwrap or undress the mummy.

Examine the material in which the mummy is wrapped. Before any type of internal study can be undertaken, textile or basketry experts are called in to examine the material encasing the mummy. The textile expert may take a microscopic snippet of material to analyze. If the material is very rare, scientists may be unable to examine the body further.

Conduct a dental examination. A thorough check of a mummy's teeth will reveal a great deal about the type of food a person ate and his health. A scientist will want to know if and how the teeth are worn down, which teeth are decayed or missing, and whether the mouth contains any signs of injury. All of this can reveal the person's diet and perhaps even show how he died. But scientists will only conduct this type of exam if the mummy's mouth is open.

Study samples of the mummy's tissues under a microscope. Called a histological exam, this allows scientists to get a closeup look at the soft tissues taken from muscles and organs. It is particularly valuable to show any diseases that the person had at the time of death. But such an examination is not always possible; it depends on the condition of the mummy and how much of it remains. Often, a mummy will be quite brittle and dry. In this case, tissues must be rehydrated (that is, mixed with a solution of water and other chemicals) to bring them back to the original condition. But scientists are unwilling to damage a mummy to retrieve any tissue samples.

Microscopic skin samples, for example, may be snipped from areas of the body that will not be on display (from its underpart, for example). Organ samples (from the lungs or liver, for example) cannot be taken if the scientist must make an incision and thereby mutilate the mummy. However, scientists are often helped by the mummymakers themselves. Sometimes they made incisions that provide today's scientists access to internal organs. Other times, they removed a person's internal organs and preserved them separately in jars or wrapped packages; samples can be taken without disturbing the mummy.

Examine the mummy's esophagus, stomach, and intestines. An endoscope, a medical tool which normally allows doctors to examine the stomach and intestines for ulcers or cancer, has most recently been used by some mummy scientists. With an endoscope, a scientist can look for signs of disease and even discover the last meal that the person ate. This examination avoids the problems associated with older methods; it does not damage the mummy since the scientist uses the mouth or rectum (the body's normal openings) as the route for the endoscope. Of course, this exam does not work with most non-Egyptian mummies whose bodies are brittle and whose mouths may be closed. In this case, a scientist might like to perform a postmortem by removing the chest plate and looking at the lungs and other internal organs. Of course, this procedure can damage the mummy severely, so it is usually not done.

Reconstruct the mummy's face. Some scientists might ask an artist to sculpt the face of the mummy to get a better sense of what the person looked like. No matter how lifelike the mummy seems, it probably does not really resemble the living person. A good artist will bring the mummy back to life with a careful and accurate reproduction of the face. As you can imagine, such an analysis takes a long time to complete. To give you a better understanding of the process, the next three chapters will describe studies undertaken by scientists to make a number of mummies share their secrets.

6. A Mummy's Tongue

Sometime during the Twentieth Dynasty of Egypt, around the year 1100 B.C., an Egyptian priest named Natsef-Amun died. As was customary at the time, his body was mummified and then placed in a tomb in an area of Egypt called Deir el Bahri. There, Natsef-Amun's mummy remained for almost 3,000 years until A.D. 1823, when M. J. Passalacqua, an "antique dealer" who was reportedly more of a grave robber, found it along with many others. Passalacqua specialized in clearing out Egyptian tombs and selling their contents.

Shortly, Natsef-Amun was offered for sale along with other items from Deir el Bahri. A group of people from Leeds, England, who had formed the Leeds Literary and Philosophical Society, arranged to buy Natsef-Amun so that they could study his remains scientifically. Members of the Leeds Society were wealthy enough to erect a museum that contained laboratories and meeting rooms. They had also hired a curator to oversee the museum's collections. Members of the museum had already studied one mummy. But when they had unwrapped it, they were dismayed to find that it had been almost entirely eaten by beetles. They hoped that Natsef-Amun's mummy would be in better condition when it arrived in Leeds in 1828. If the outer coffin that enclosed it was any indication, they were not going to be disappointed.

Natsef-Amun's body was enclosed in two coffins. The outer one was constructed of sycamore, in the shape of a man with his arms crossed on his chest. The face, however, did not belong to Natsef-Amun. At the time of his death, pre-made coffins with standard male and female faces carved on the outer coffin were sold. Only members of the royal families had coffins tailored to their own likeness.

The coffin's yellow background was decorated along the sides with about thirty scenes from Egyptian mythology. According to A. Rosalie David and Edmund Tapp, who have studied Natsef-Amun both inside and out and who have published their findings in a book entitled *A Mummy's Tale,* the scenes were a kind of magical protection for Natsef-Amun that would enable him to reach the underworld.

Soon after the mummy arrived in Leeds, members of the society conducted an autopsy on it. After removing the body from the coffins, they began to unwind the linen wrappings. They discovered that Natsef-Amun was wrapped in at least forty layers of linen. As was common, the outer wrappings were made of excellent-quality, finely woven narrow linen. But the cloth became increasingly coarser and wider for the inner wrappings. Between some of the wrappings, jewelry and ornaments were found. The last layer of bandages did not reveal Natsef-Amun's face or body immediately, since a one-inch layer of spices had been placed between the skin and the linen. The spices had also been used to fill the abdominal and chest cavities. His mouth and throat were also filled with a powder made from vegetables, and his cheeks were filled with sawdust to maintain the natural shape of the face.

On that day in 1828, almost three thousand years after Natsef-Amun's death, the autopsy team could smell cinnamon in the air around them as they removed the last layer of bandages. When the spices were removed, they saw the body of a priest: his head, eyebrows, and beard had been shaved. William Osburn, one member of the autopsy team, noted that his skin was gray, in good condition, and "soft and greasy to touch."

The team inspected him carefully and saw that the embalmers had used a classic and very elaborate method of mummification. They had removed his internal organs, treated them with a saltlike substance called natron, put them into packages, and replaced them in his abdomen. The brain had been removed (as was common in the process of mummification used at the time of his death) through the right nostril. The inside of the skull had been filled with powdered spices.

Perhaps the team's most striking discovery was the fact that Natsef-Amun's tongue was sticking out of his mouth. This was quite unusual; only one other mummy

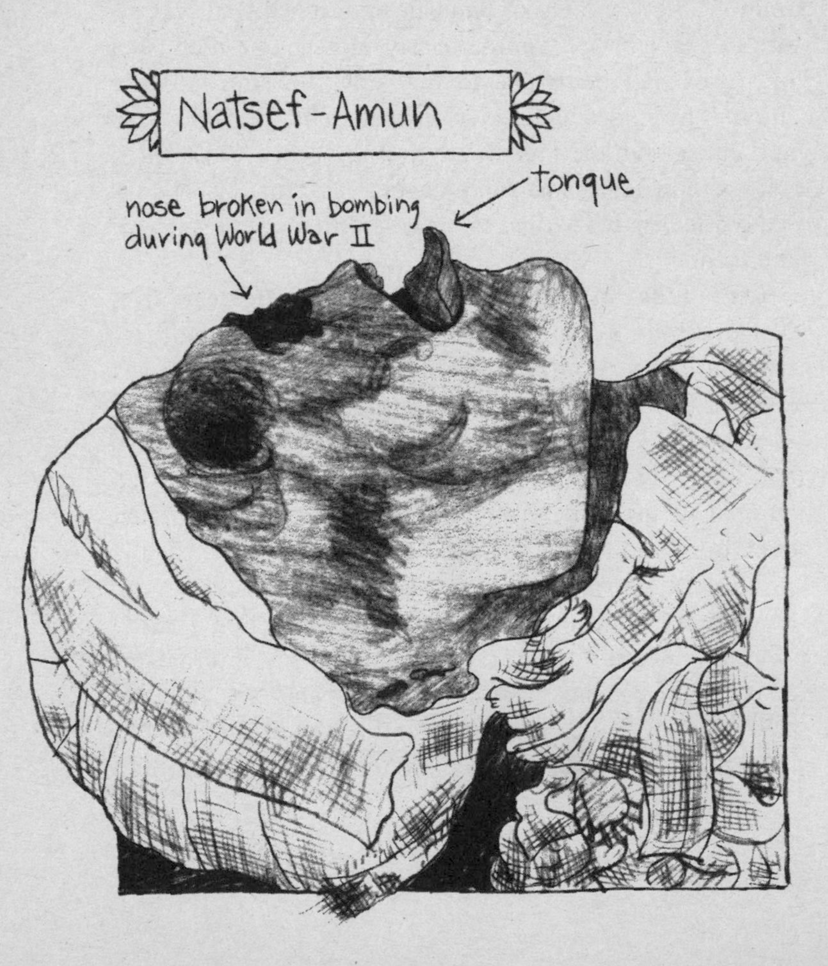

has ever been discovered with this feature. No one could decide if this bizarre quality was related to his death. Although the autopsy suggested that he had died at middle age, the nineteenth-century scientists had no idea what had caused his death.

After the autopsy, Natsef-Amun was kept on display with other mummies at the Leeds City Museum. On March 15, 1941, the mummy collection was damaged by a German bomb. His nose was broken off and the lid of his inner coffin was smashed. Still, Natsef-Amun was fortunate, since all of the other mummies in the Leeds City Museum were completely destroyed by the blast.

Despite the 1828 autopsy, many questions about Natsef-Amun remained unanswered. In 1989, members of the Manchester Egyptian Mummy Research Project, headed by Dr. A. Rosalie David, were asked to conduct a second autopsy. Over 160 years, great refinements had been made in medical science, even medical science applied to mummies. The Manchester team was chosen to study Natsef-Amun since it used nondestructive techniques.

The team used many methods to study Natsef-Amun. Of course, they were curious to know what caused his tongue to protrude. On closer examination, they discovered that his tongue appeared to have broken off sometime during the mummification process. The embalmers then covered it with glue so that it might be reattached. But this didn't explain why his tongue protruded.

The team considered three possibilities:

1. Natsef-Amun had a tumor.
2. Natsef-Amun was strangled.
3. Natsef-Amun had been stung on his tongue by a bee, which caused him to choke to death.

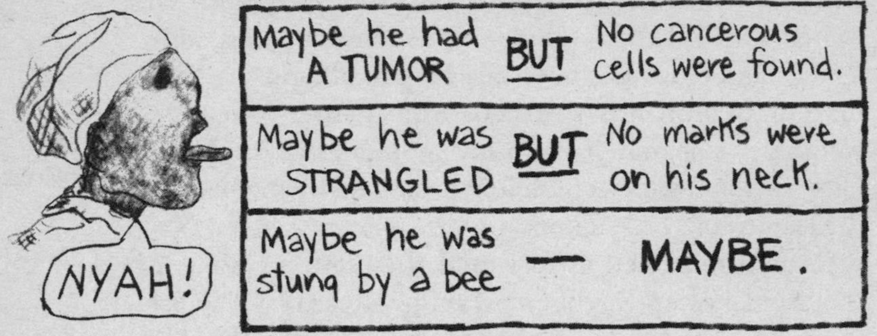

THE MYSTERY of NATSEF-AMUN'S TONGUE
Maybe he had A TUMOR
BUT
No cancerous cells were found.
Maybe he was STRANGLED
BUT
No marks were on his neck.
Maybe he was stung by a bee
— MAYBE.
NYAH!

The Manchester team ruled out the first two possibilities. The tongue appeared to be no larger than normal; when the scientists looked at cells from it under a microscope, they did not find any cancerous ones. They also ruled out the possibility that he was strangled, since his neck had no marks whatsoever.

That left the possibility of a bee sting or some other type of allergic reaction. Because bodily fluids were drained from the body during mummification, there was no way to check for an allergy. Although the Manchester team could not reach a definite conclusion, this possibility could not be ruled out.

MUMMY FINDER: Natsef-Amun's mummy is currently on display at the Leeds City Museum, Leeds, England.

7. A Mummy's Tummy

Maybe Andy Mould had a special knack that most people don't have. Or maybe it was just a coincidence. But in 1983 and then again in 1984, he found human remains in an English peat bog known as Lindow Moss. The first time, he had found the head (mostly a skull with little skin or brain remaining) of a woman.

A year later, on August 1, 1984, he was working with Eddie Slack, placing blocks of peat onto an elevator that would transport them to a shredding mill, when he looked at one block of peat and noticed what he thought was a piece of wood embedded in it. He threw it toward Eddie but it struck the ground and crumbled, revealing a human foot. Without hesitation, Andy reported his disturbing find, and shortly the police arrived. With Andy and Eddie's help, they located the area of the bog where the foot had been found. There, on the surface, was a flap of darkened skin belonging to what was later called Lindow Man. They covered it with wet peat until scientists could be summoned to view the body.

Five days later, in the presence of several paleobotanists and a biologist, the block of peat containing Lindow Man was cut, placed on a sheet of plywood, and transported to a local hospital. There, the authorities attempted to date the remains. After all, no one knew if Lindow Man was a recent murder victim or a man from the past.

As it turned out, Lindow Man had died between A.D. 50 and A.D. 100. The scientists learned, when the body was examined, that the man had been murdered. They determined this by examining his body visually and then inspecting x-rays of it. At the same time, they tried to create an image of Lindow Man's appearance. Then they looked inside — especially at his stomach — to find more clues to the mystery of his death.

Step 1: Examining Lindow Man Visually

A close visual examination provided obvious clues that Lindow Man had been murdered.

Head and neck. First, he had been hit twice on the crown of his head with a blunt object, probably an ax; he had also been struck once at the base of his skull. Second, he had been strangled. Around Lindow Man's neck

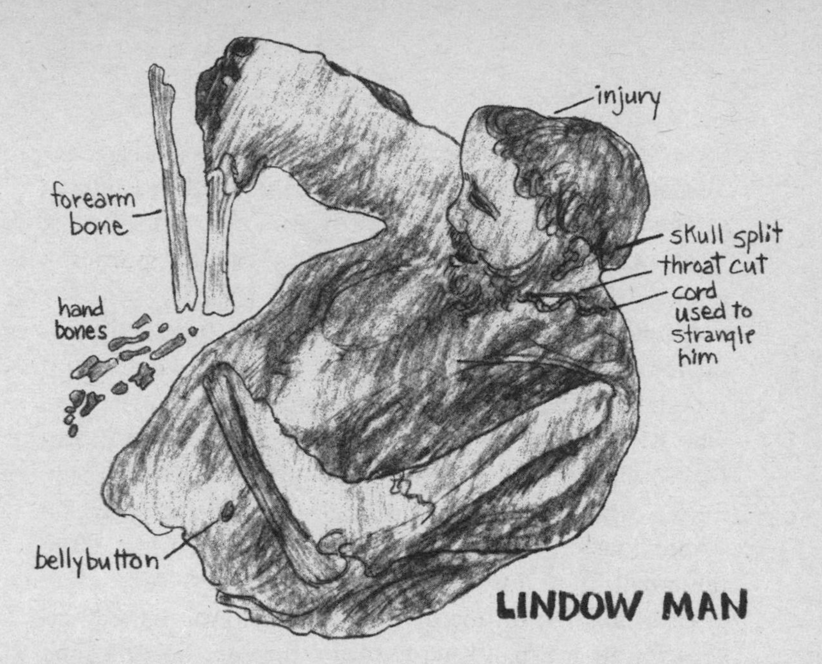

was a small rope that had been twisted tightly, closing off his windpipe and breaking two of his neck vertebrae. Finally, scientists found a gash at the throat, which may indicate that his throat was cut, though some scientists think that the wound occurred naturally after his death. If indeed his throat was cut, it was probably done to drain his body of blood.

Hair. Scientists discovered some interesting details by looking at Lindow Man's hair and beard. They were surprised that he had a beard, since no other male bog body had been found with a beard; this was clearly not common at the time he lived. Scientists also learned that someone had trimmed Lindow Man's hair with scissors two or three days before his death. Historians and archaeologists knew that, although scissors existed in England at the time, they would have been uncommon, most likely reserved for a privileged few. Was the murdered man, they wondered, a dignitary?

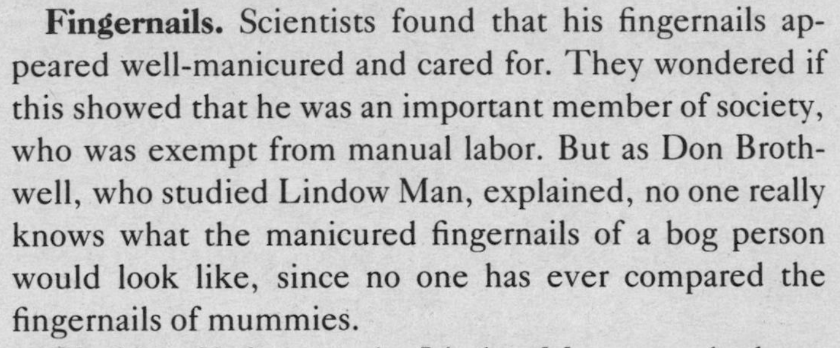

Fingernails. Scientists found that his fingernails appeared well-manicured and cared for. They wondered if this showed that he was an important member of society, who was exempt from manual labor. But as Don Brothwell, who studied Lindow Man, explained, no one really knows what the manicured fingernails of a bog person would look like, since no one has ever compared the fingernails of mummies.

Clothing. Unfortunately, Lindow Man was naked, except for an arm band made of fox fur and the thin rope around his neck. Without clothes, he could have been a king or a laborer. As author Brothwell put it:

> Why did he have a well-developed, but roughly trimmed, beard — unique among bog bodies — and well-kept nails? Was he an aristocrat fallen on hard times, or a high-born prisoner sacrificed to the gods?

Step 2: Reconstructing Lindow Man

The next step pursued was the reconstruction of Lindow Man. What did he look like? How tall was he? What was his body build? Because his body was rather flattened and his face squashed by the layers of heavy peat bog pressing against the body, scientists wanted to get a more realistic picture of the 2,000-year-old man.

Height. Forensic anthropologists and other scientists can use the length of a person's leg bones (the femur and tibia) to provide an estimate of his height. Remember, though, that Lindow Man's legs had not been recovered with the body. The scientists had to use another technique which relied on the humerus (or upper arm bone). In this way, they determined that Lindow Man was about five feet seven inches tall, probably a little taller than most men in his realm.

Appearance. Some of the scientists made a clay model of Lindow Man's facc. This is what he may have looked like:

Body build. The team of scientists noted that, judging from the outside anyway, Lindow Man was well-built and clearly in his prime.

Step 3: Exploring Lindow Man's Stomach

When the scientists explored Lindow Man's interior cavity, looking for any signs of disease, they were pleased to find that his stomach had not decayed. It contained something like brown mud, the remnants of the last meal he had eaten. Because they found only twenty grams of partially digested food, the scientists concluded that Lindow Man's last meal was really more of a snack. It consisted mostly of cereal grains, but something that he ate was burnt. They wondered, was it bread or gruel? Although no one can be certain, they believe that his meal consisted in part of some charred bread (though he could have had some scorched gruel, too).

They also found evidence of pollen from a mistletoe plant in his stomach. If it came from a flower, this would allow scientists to place his death in March or April. If it was dried pollen, added as an ingredient to his dinner, then the time of his death is harder to place.

HOW POLLEN GRAINS LOOK THROUGH A MICROSCOPE

Archaeologist Anne Ross thinks she knows what happened to Lindow Man. When the Romans invaded Britain, they conquered the local tribes of Celts and wrote a number of accounts describing Celtic ceremonies and practices, many of which struck them as barbaric. In one festival, called Beltain, which was held on May 1, a victim was selected for sacrifice to make surc that the summer's crops would be successful.

Here's how historians believe the festival was celebrated: a bonfire was lit on top of a hill. In it, an oatmeal cake, called a bannock, was baked and a small portion of it charred. The bannock was then broken into small pieces and put in a bag. The person who chose the burnt piece of bannock became the sacrificial victim. Ross believes that Lindow Man was a Beltain sacrifice.

Historians, though, have pointed out that the victim selected during Beltain was almost always burned in the bonfire. So how, if Lindow Man was a Beltain victim, did he escape the fire and find his way to the bog?

According to Ross, the Celts considered the number three holy. They had three gods: Taranis, the god of thunder; Esus, the god of the underworld; and Teutates, the god of the tribe. Each required a specific type of sacrifice. Ross explains:

> Taranis required prisoners of war to be burnt alive in giant wicker cages, while Esus was offered victims who were either hanged from sacred trees or stabbed to death or both. Teutates, however, took his sacrifices into a watery embrace in the sacred wells and pools that always figured very strongly among Celtic holy sites.

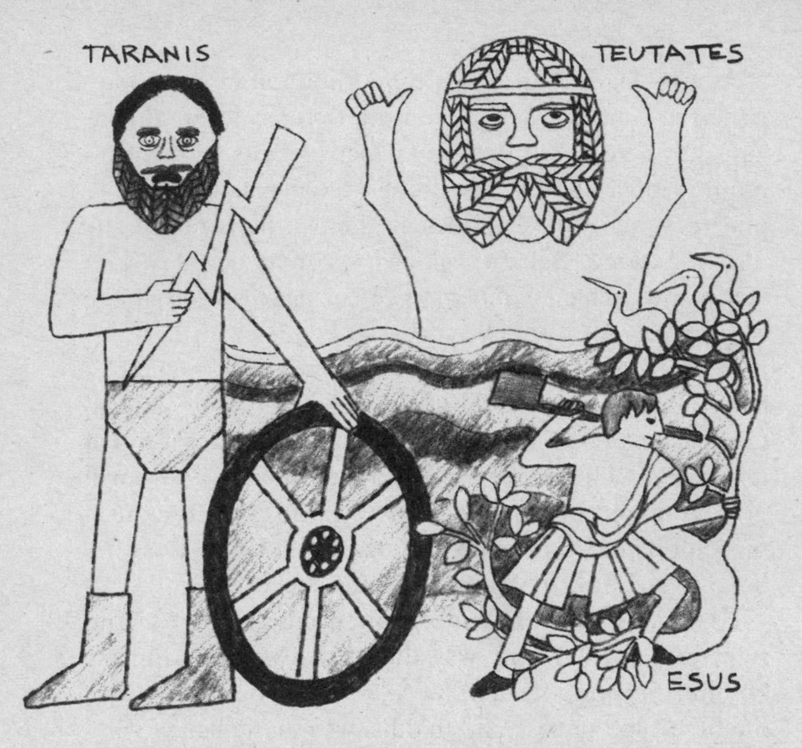

Instead of sacrificing three individuals, the Celts sometimes sacrificed one person to please all three gods. This could have been the case with Lindow Man. First, he was sacrificed to Taranis. Although normally involving fire, sacrifices to Taranis were also made with the use of a weapon. In the case of Lindow Man, the three blows to his skull, writes Ross, were "delivered with the sudden awful force of a thunderbolt, the mark of Taranis." Second, he was sacrificed to Esus when he was strangled and his throat cut. Third, he was sacrificed to Teutates when he was placed in the bog and drowned.

But who was Lindow Man, and why was he sacrificed in such an elaborate ceremony? Although victims might have been sacrificed occasionally, they were not usually killed the way Lindow Man was. Had it simply been the bad luck of selecting the charred piece of bannock? Or was more involved?

Ross concludes that he was either a Celtic priest, otherwise known as a Druid, or a king. Because his hands were free from calluses and his body had not previously been injured, he was neither a laborer nor a warrior. He was clearly an important man — not the type of person routinely sacrificed.

Ross guesses that the invasion of the Romans in A.D. 43 may have caused the Celts to take the dramatic step of sacrificing an extremely important individual in their attempt to appease the gods and thwart the Romans. In fact, she goes so far as to place his death in A.D. 60, after the Romans had attempted to wipe out all traces of the Celts and the Druids. She believes that Lindow Man may even have chosen to die himself in order "to stave off the Roman threat." Whether or not Ross's speculations are correct, they provide an interesting theory. They also show how much — and how little — scientists can learn from a mummy's tummy.

Since at least portions of two other bog bodies have been found in Lindow Moss — and since thousands

Details from a scene on the Gunderstrup Cauldron found in Denmark. It shows a sacrifice of warriors who are greeted by the Dog of Death. The men on horseback may represent the new glory earned by those sacrificed.

have been found in bogs over the years — scientists are likely to have many more opportunities to study the mysteries that bog bodies present.

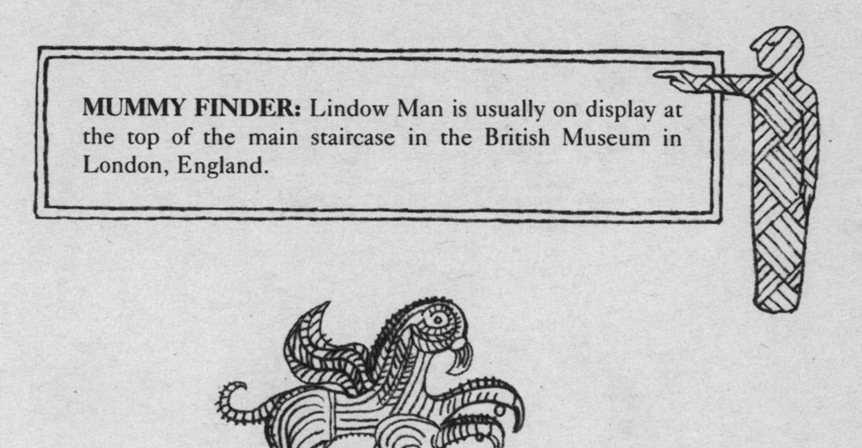

MUMMY FINDER: Lindow Man is usually on display at the top of the main staircase in the British Museum in London, England.

8. Three Mummies' Tales

One of the most interesting cases involving frozen remains began about one hundred and fifty years ago with an expedition to find the Northwest Passage, a sea route to Asia, by traveling around the northern edge of North America.

On May 19, 1845, Sir John Franklin and his 134-man crew sailed from Greenhithe, England, in two ships, the HMS *Terror* and the *Erebus*. Franklin envisioned a lengthy and difficult trip through Arctic waters, so the ships were specially prepared and outfitted. The ships had steam heat (to keep the crew warm), locomotive-driven propellers (to provide power if the ships became stuck in the ice), and iron-reinforced bows (to help the ships cut through ice floes). They were so well stocked with food (including more than 120,000 pounds of flour, almost 17,000 liters of alcohol, and about 8,000 tin cans

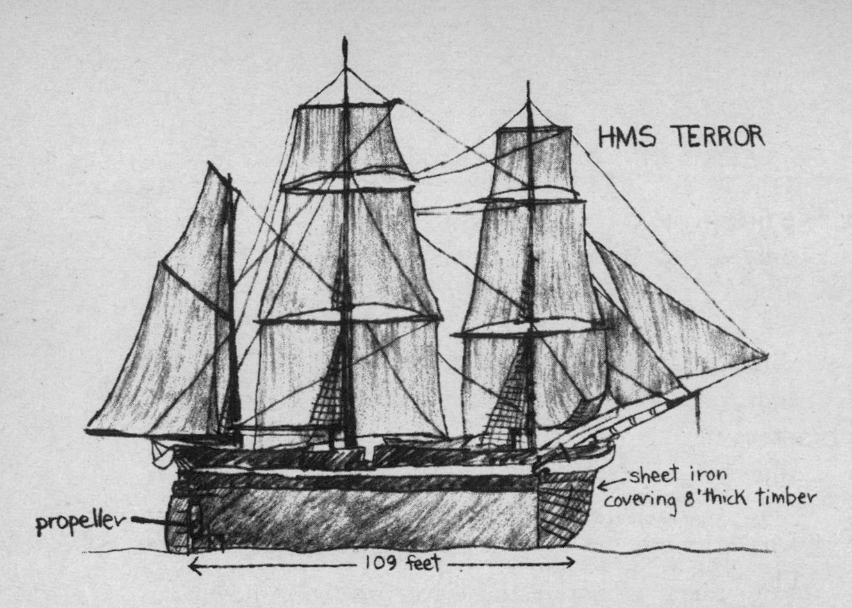

of meat, soup, and vegetables) that Franklin believed he had enough to last five — and maybe seven — years. The ships even had room for some luxuries, such as extensive libraries, hand organs, mahogany writing desks, and school supplies that could be used to teach reading and writing to crew members.

Once the ships reached Baffin Bay in late July, however, no one heard from Franklin or his crew again. Approximately twenty-five major search expeditions were needed to uncover some of the facts surrounding what became known as "the Franklin disaster."

An 1850 expedition seemed to promise some answers when Captain Erasmus Ommanney came across the ruins of a stone hut, cans of food, torn mittens — and the graves of three of Franklin's crew. Headboards indicated that the men had died separately, from unknown causes. The first to die was John Torrington, on January 1, 1846 — only seven months into the expedition. The other headboards marked the graves of John Hartnell, who died four days after Torrington, and William Braine, who died three months later. Rather than explain anything, though, the burial site simply added to the puzzle: why had the crew begun to die so early in the expedition?

Another expedition in 1857, led by Sir Francis McClintock, discovered a number of written messages which did provide some answers. The *Erebus* and *Terror* had become stuck in the ice in September 1846. During the next year and a half, nine officers, including Sir John Franklin, and fifteen sailors died. Finally, in April 1848, the surviving members of the expedition decided to abandon the ships and walk on the ice some 120 miles to a river where they could row to a trading post. The unfinished messages suggested that none had survived, and it is easy to see why: the men used extremely poor judgment. Not only had they tried to drag a 1,200-pound lifeboat across the ice, they had selected an assortment of strange items to fill the boat: silk handkerchiefs, perfumed soap, six books, tea, and chocolate.

Despite their importance, the messages failed to explain *why* the expedition had failed. The answer to the mystery, a doctor on one of the search trips surmised, might be found by examining the bodies of Torrington, Hartnell, and Braine to look for clues to the cause of their deaths. But his idea struck authorities as improper, and it was ignored. Finally, in 1980, anthropologist Owen Beattie decided to study the remains of the three men to "look for information on health and diet, for indications of disease, for evidence of violence, and information as to each individual's age and stature." Beattie was going to solve the mystery — even if it meant examining three frozen mummies.

The First Autopsy

On August 17, 1984, Beattie and his research team were ready to examine John Torrington at the gravesite on Beechey Island. To get this far, the team had had to dig six feet through the icy earth to Torrington's frozen coffin. Then they had to remove the last layer of ice from the top of the coffin. As they did, they became aware of a strong odor — not from Torrington's body but from the blue wool cloth that covered the coffin. Even after 138 years, the cloth reeked.

As Beattie and his crew came closer to the coffin lid, he and journalist John Geiger wrote that

> the wind picked up dramatically and a massive, black thunder cloud moved over the site. The walls of the tent covering the excavation began to snap loudly, and as the weather continued to worsen the five researchers finally stopped their work and looked at one another. . . . Some of the crew were visibly

nervous and Beattie decided to call a halt to work for the day. That night the wind howled continuously, rattling the sides of Beattie's tent all night and sometimes smacking its folds against his face, making sleep difficult.

The next morning the winds had died down; Beattie was finally able to remove the last covering of ice and gravel stuck to the top of the coffin. When the coffin top was completely open, Beattie and his team were confronted by a block of ice that contained Torrington's body.

Now they had to determine how to thaw the body from the ice. They could not use any hot air, since that might destroy the body and any artifacts. They couldn't wait for the body to thaw on its own, because the outside air temperature was below freezing. And they could not chip at the ice for fear of damaging the body.

They decided to pour water onto the ice, section by section. The first part to be revealed was Torrington's shirt, then his bare white toes. A piece of the blue fabric that had covered the coffin also covered Torrington's face. Team member Arne Carlson worked on thawing the cloth so that it could be moved without tearing and shredding it. He worked with warm water and large surgical tweezers to free the fabric from the ice.

Suddenly the last bit of ice fell away and the fabric lifted free. Torrington — only twenty at the time of his death — looked peaceful. His eyes were partially open; the skin on his nose and forehead had been darkened by

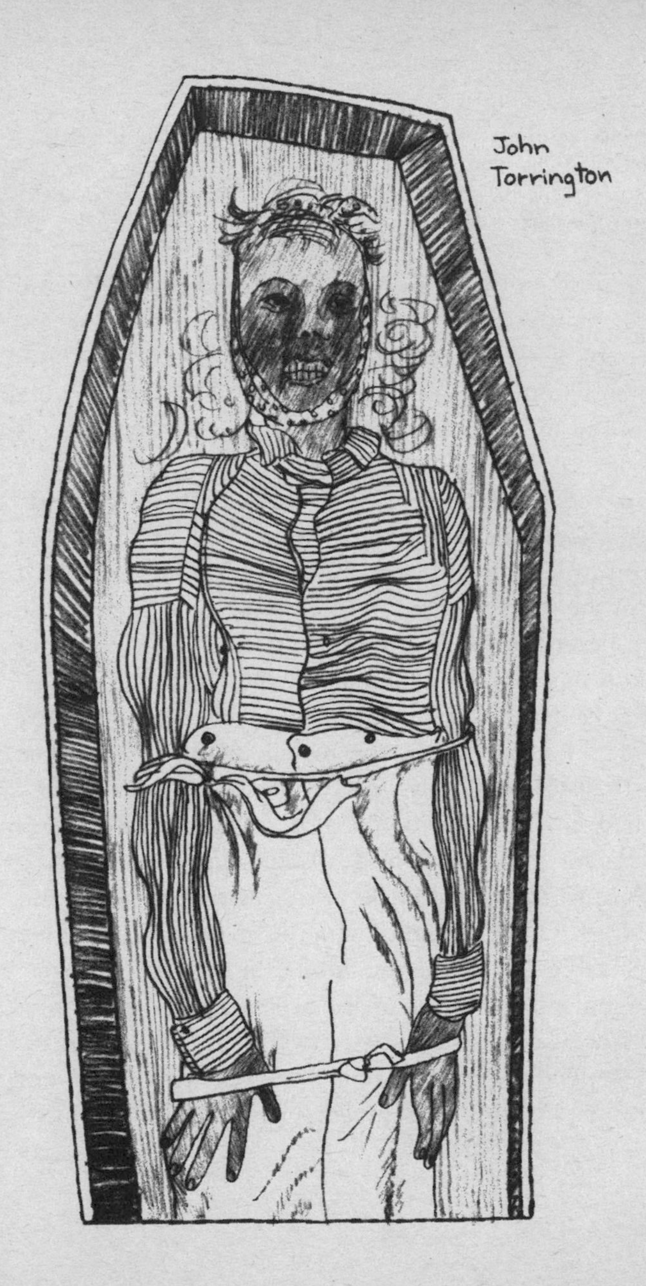
John
Torrington

the blue cloth. The rest of his face was quite pale. His teeth were clenched, his lips open.

The thawing of the entire body continued, so that it could be autopsied. When the ice was gone, Beattie and Carlson picked John Torrington's body up from the coffin. Rather than the stiff body they had expected, they found it to be limp.

When the researchers undressed Torrington, they discovered how sick he had really been. His body was so thin that each rib was clearly visible; he weighed only about 85 pounds. Though Torrington's body would have lost weight and shrunk due to the fact that its moisture began to evaporate once he died, Beattie concluded he had been thin and frail at the time of his death. His hands were callus-free; his nails were clean. Although he was the head stoker of the *Terror*, Torrington obviously had been too sick to work for a long time before his death.

The autopsy process, which involved the removal of tissue and organ samples, bone cuttings, and fingernail and hair clippings, took four hours. When they were finished, the men had little time left before they were scheduled to be picked up by a small plane to escape the onset of the early Arctic winter. They quickly visited the site of a large tin can dump used by Franklin's men during their stay on the island. Beattie examined some cans — still there after 138 years — and removed a few to study later. Then the team returned to civilization to analyze their findings.

The autopsy results showed that Torrington suffered from a variety of lung problems caused by smoking or by breathing coal dust. He appeared to have died of pneumonia. But this condition was aggravated by a surprising condition: a high exposure to lead. This fact was discovered by analyzing a ten-centimeter length of Torrington's hair taken from the back of his neck. Microscopic examination of this hair revealed that Torrington had ingested large quantities of lead during the first eight months of the expedition.

Beattie wanted to know where the lead had come from. He examined the tin cans from the island and found that they were improperly soldered, which would have allowed lead to leak into the food. Could this have been responsible, he wondered, for the deaths of all the men?

Two More Autopsies

Two summers later, Beattie returned with a team of ten researchers. This time the group would be performing autopsies on Hartnell and Braine — and taking x-rays of their bodies. If they found evidence of lead poisoning, Beattie would be close to confirming his suspicions. Following the same process they had used on Torrington, the team uncovered and then thawed the two bodies.

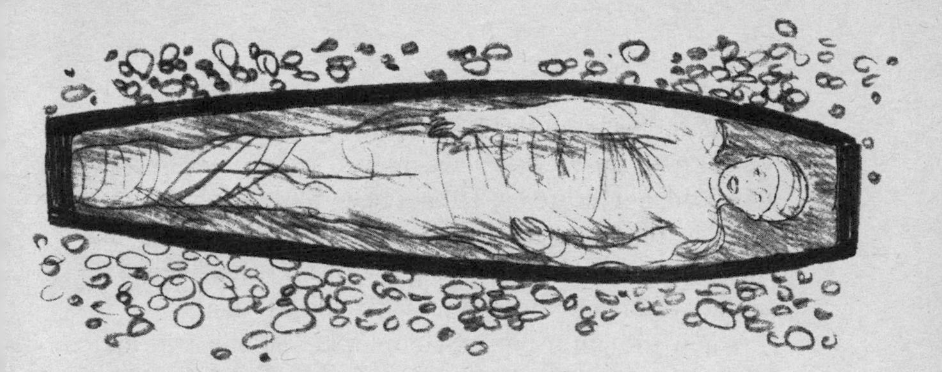

Hartnell's body held a surprise for the team: it had already been autopsied, most likely by Harry Goodsir, the doctor on board the *Erebus*. By looking at the type of incision and noting the organs that had been removed, Beattie and his team realized what Goodsir had concluded: Hartnell had died of tuberculosis. Nonetheless, Beattie took samples of Hartnell's tissues, hair, fingernails, bones, and organs.

The team was also surprised by Braine's body. His face was covered by a bright red handkerchief. When it was removed, Beattie and the others saw a grinning mouth and a flattened nose. Because the coffin had not been quite deep enough, the coffin lid had pressed into Braine's nose when it was sealed. Although his eyeballs weren't well preserved, his half-opened eyes and glassy eyeballs made him look as if he had just woken from a long nap.

Unexpectedly, they found that his left arm had been amputated and placed under the body. Examination also revealed teeth marks on his shoulders and other parts of the body: his body had been gnawed on by rats before it was buried. In fact, his body showed signs of decomposition, which indicated it had not been buried immediately after death, but had been exposed to the elements and the rats for a while. That might explain the evidence of his hasty burial (and the removal of his left arm).

When the autopsy was completed and the two men reburied, Beattie and his team left the island. All of the samples that they took were sent away for analysis, and Beattie anxiously waited for the results.

The Final Results

The labs confirmed what Beattie expected: high lead levels in all three men. Unquestionably, their exposure to lead had come from the tinned food that had made up so much of the crew's nourishment. Then, as now, government contracts were awarded to the lowest bidder. The company that had supplied the canned goods had a reputation for producing inferior goods. And although the three men had not died of lead poisoning itself, their exposure to such high amounts of lead weakened them to the point that other diseases could take hold and eventually kill them. As for the remaining crew, their reasoning powers had been damaged — fatally, one might say — by their exposure to lead. The 120-mile march across the ice with the heavy lifeboat and irrelevant goods was proof of that.

The problems of lead poisoning were not well known in 1845, and it wasn't until 1890 that soldering the inside of food cans was banned in England — forty-five years after the Franklin expedition. Nonetheless, the mystery of the disastrous expedition was explained quite clearly by the mummies of three of its crew members.

tin can fragment found to contain lead

Part III
How to Make a Mummy Happy

9. Stopping Mummy Dummies

Knowing how mummies are made and how scientists study them is only part of understanding mummies. It's also important to know how they have been used and misused by others. Because mummies are usually considered curiosities, they have been treated with disrespect. It's enough to make a mummy (or a daddy) cry.

Mummy Dummy 1: Grave Robbers

Originally, the main source of trouble for mummies was plunderers, who robbed graves looking for jewelry and other valuables. Rather than respect the dead, these individuals looked upon mummies as obstacles (in which case, they destroyed them) or as treasure chests (in which case, they would literally rip the mummy apart looking for jewelry). Sometimes grave robbers sold or used mummies for unexpected purposes.

For example, when Mark Twain visited Egypt in the late nineteenth century, he discovered a unique use of mummies. A railroad was being built to cross Egypt, and workers used mummies as fuel for the engine rather than coal. Since they were often coated or filled with bitumen or pitch (a coal-like substance), they probably burned quite well. Twain joked, though, that he heard an engineer curse the mummies of common people who "don't burn worth a cent! Pass out a King!" No one knows if one type burned better than others, however, and Twain's account of mummies used as fuel is the only one in existence. What's more, no one knows how many mummies were destroyed in this way.

Another strange use of mummies was dreamed up by the industrialist Augustus Stanwood, who bought tons of the cloth used to wrap mummies so that he could make paper in Maine. Because there were many mummies available and because each one might be wrapped in twenty pounds of cloth or more, Stanwood thought he had found a perfect way to make a lot of money. The problem, wrote author Christine El Mahdy, was that the cloth was so discolored, Stanwood couldn't make white paper from it. He resorted to making brown wrapping paper. His plan was halted, however, when a cholera epidemic broke out and people mistakenly thought that Stanwood's "mummy paper" was to blame.

Sometimes grave robbers got their just deserts, too. One party of treasureseekers came across a tomb near some pyramids in Egypt around 1800, according to E. A. Wallis Budge. In it, they found a sealed jar that contained honey. Greedily, they began to eat the honey by dipping bread into it. Perhaps they thought that centuries-old honey might provide a splendid feast. One of the plunderers noticed a hair on top of the honey after they had eaten some. He tried to pull it out, but was surprised to find that something was attached to it. He pulled the hair firmly and up from the jar came the body of a fully dressed child, who had obviously been preserved in the honey.

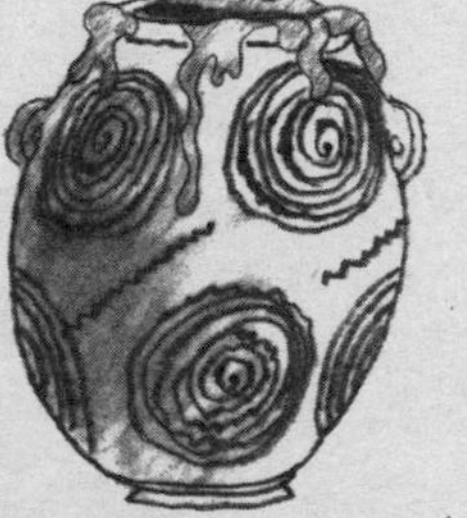

Mummy Dummy 2: Medieval Doctors and Their Patients

During the Middle Ages, many people came to believe that mummies had a medicinal value, especially those covered with bitumen or pitch. According to Christine El Mahdy, a medieval doctor in Cairo wrote that bitumen could be taken internally or applied to the outside of the body. But, he noted, if getting bitumen is a problem, "corpses may be substituted."

By the twelfth century, mummy powder was prescribed for wounds and bruises. But it became important to distinguish among the various kinds of mummies. El Mahdy says that Egyptian doctors classified a mummy as one of four types:

1. Egyptian mummies preserved in bitumen
2. Artificial Egyptian mummies (made from bitumen and herbs but containing no body)
3. Arabic mummies (preserved in oils and spices but containing no bitumen)
4. Bodies buried and dried in the sand.

The bodies buried and dried in the sand were the least useful to doctors; such bodies were pulverized and used to relieve upset stomachs.

The first three types of mummies became a big business, however. Thousands of Egyptian mummies preserved in bitumen were ground up and sold as medicine. By the 1500s, though, the supply of mummies ran short and the bodies of executed criminals and deceased hospital patients were substituted. Merchants went so far, notes author Carol Andrews, as to bury the recently deceased in the sand to dry them out or to stuff them with bitumen and dry them in the sun. Egyptologist E. A. Wallis Budge wrote in his classic book *The Mummy:*

> In the year 1564 a physician called Guy de la Fontaine made an attempt to see the stock of mummies of the chief merchant of mummies at Alexandria [Egypt], and he discovered that they were made from the bodies of slaves and others who had died from the most loathsome diseases. The traffic in mummies as a drug was stopped in a curious manner.

Not content to ransack Egyptian tombs for mummies, merchants turned to sources like the Canary Islands, off the northwest coast of Africa. The Guanche people once practiced mummymaking on these islands. After Spain invaded the Canary Islands in 1402, thousands of mummies were found in caves scattered across Tenerife, the largest island. It appeared that most of them had belonged to the Guanche aristocracy.

In 1526, a man named Thomas Nichols explored a cave containing approximately four hundred mummies. Many of the mummies were lying in the extended position, but some were standing straight up and others were hanging from the walls. In 1770, a cave containing 1,000 mummies was located between the towns of Arico and Guimar. And in 1773, a smaller mummy cave was found by a Captain Young who commanded the sloop *Weasel.* In this cave, the mummies were sewn up in goat skins. Young asked the local priest if he could buy one of the bodies. At first, the priest objected, but when Young offered him some gold, the priest allowed him to buy one. Young took the mummy back to England and presented it to Trinity College, Cambridge.

In all, five caves on Tenerife holding mummies were found, though some accounts reveal that at least twenty caves existed. Despite the number of mummies that were discovered on Tenerife, almost none are in existence today because most were turned into powder and sold as medicine. Those placed on display in museums have been removed from exhibit recently; therefore, it is no longer possible to see a Guanche mummy except in a photograph or illustration.

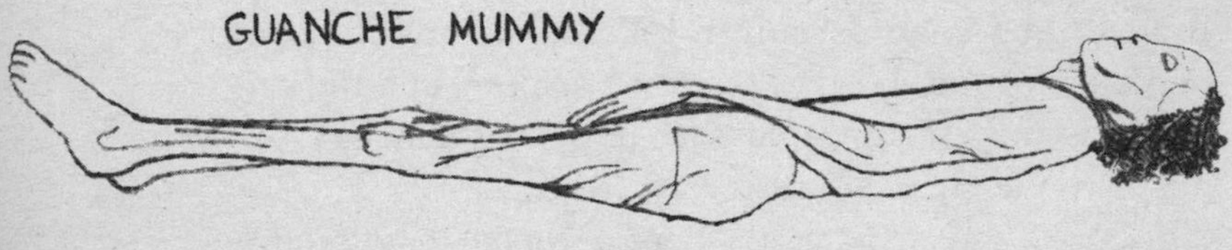

GUANCHE MUMMY

Mummy Dummy 3: Treasure Hunters and Antique Collectors

Archaeology wasn't always the science that it is today. In the late 1800s, there weren't any textbooks or professors to teach interested persons how to study or even safeguard their discoveries. Often, these "archaeologists" were more like treasure hunters or antiques dealers; they hunted for ancient tombs or burial grounds, often with the good intention of preserving what they had found.

Sometimes they kept the contents of the tombs (including any mummies) themselves; sometimes they sold them, especially to museums interested in adding to their collections. Unfortunately, many mummies were lost or destroyed in the process.

For example, Giovanni Belzoni, an engineer who achieved great success as a circus strongman, was hired in 1817 as an agent of the British Museum to acquire antiquities in Egypt. Four years later, he published an account of his work, describing what happened to some mummies he discovered in the tombs at Gournou in 1817. He had followed winding passages within one

GIOVANNI BELZONI

tomb and was so tired that he wanted to find a place to sit down and rest. Unfortunately, he decided to sit on a mummy, and it collapsed from his weight. He recalled:

> I sunk altogether among the broken mummies, with a crash of bones, rags, and wooden cases, which raised such a dust as kept me motionless for a quarter of an hour, waiting till it subsided again. I could not [leave] the place, however, without increasing it, and every step I took I crushed a mummy in some part or other.

In one narrow tomb passage, which was "choked with mummies,"

> I could not pass without putting my face in contact with that of some decayed Egyptian; but as the passage inclined downward, my own weight helped me on; however, I could not avoid being covered with bones, legs, arms, and heads rolling from above. Thus I proceeded from one [tomb] to another, all full of mummies piled up in various ways, some standing, some lying, and some on their heads.

Although Belzoni uncovered many royal tombs, including one of the best royal mummies ever found, Seti I, he also managed to destroy many mummies in the process.

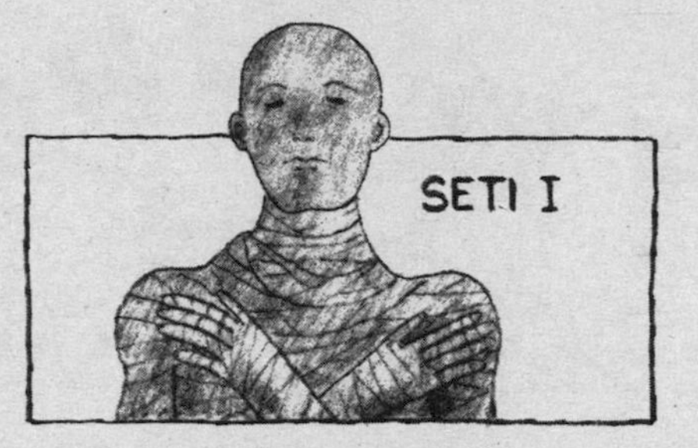

Don't assume that this type of mummy dummy no longer exists. In the southwestern United States, archaeologists frequently encounter damage to Native American sites done by "pot hunters." These pillagers ransack ancient burial grounds, dismembering and destroying the human remains in their quest for Indian pottery to sell. Even though such looting is a federal crime, pot hunters seem to stop at nothing, even grave robbing, to make money.

Sometimes, however, there is a fine line between pot hunting and preserving the past. This was the case when the Mesa Verde ruins in southwest Colorado were explored by the Wetherill brothers in the early 1900s. The Wetherills tried to get the United States government to help in preserving the ruins and their contents, but the government wasn't interested at the time. So the Wetherills went to work.

Besides baskets and tools, they found a number of Indian mummies, or, in the words of Benjamin Alfred Wetherill, "the dried-up remains of a people without a name." They put the mummies, along with other artifacts, on tour — first in Colorado, then in Minneapolis and Chicago — so that people could see "who was who in Colorado in prehistoric times." Of course, the objects and remains did not come from prehistoric times, archaeologists discovered sometime later; rather, they were no more than 1,000 years old. But the Wetherills did the best they could to promote an interest in the past and to make sure that most of the items were placed in museums.

They were quite moved by what they discovered in the ruined cliff dwellings. One infant mummy was photographed, and this poem was written about it by Benjamin Wetherill:

Greetings, child of an ancient race.
How little is told by thy baby face
Of children's joys and a mother's tears
All lost now for a thousand years.

Thy once bright eyes beheld great things.
Thou hope of parents that childhood brings.
Yet thou, with others of thy race,
Were doomed to pass; leave but a trace.

None there are who can thy story tell.
All are gone where thou didst dwell.
All voices stilled; all lips are sealed
Forever closed and unrevealed.

His brother Richard made a stunning discovery one night in January 1897 as he excavated a site near Green Marsh Spring. Writer David Roberts describes the find that he made working by lantern light:

> A 66-inch-wide basket covered another; under them lay a turkey-feather blanket decorated with bluebird feathers, and another blanket spangled with canary yellow spots. A final basket covered the perfectly mummified head of a woman. Her body was painted yellow, her face red.

Wetherill called her "the Princess." She, too, was put on exhibit.

Although the Wetherills' intentions were honest and heartfelt, in later years many people came to believe that the display of Native American mummies was demeaning and disrespectful. Recently, laws were passed by Congress preventing the exhibition of Native American mummies and allowing their return to various tribes for burial. Even the artifacts recovered at archaeological sites are often returned to tribes, because they are viewed as sacred objects.

Mummy Dummy 4: Mummy Magicians

In the past, some mummy dummies thought they were quite clever. They believed that people would flock anywhere to see a mummy. They also thought they would become rich. So some people became "mummy magicians" and conjured up mummies out of thin air.

For example, many Native American mummies were supposedly discovered in the area surrounding Mammoth Cave in Kentucky. Some, those from Mammoth Cave itself, really were found there; others, reported by owners of nearby caves, were clearly hoaxes. But these false mummies were often advertised in hopes that large numbers of people would pay money to visit the smaller caves. The author Angelo George wrote that one cave was said to hold the mummies of a man and woman

> dressed in Roman costume, and each holding in the arms a child — the man one of 10 years, and the woman a babe of 1 or 2 years. . . . A petrified monkey, as perfect in shape as if alive, was [also] found in the cave.

Other caves in the area reportedly had mummies *and* Egyptian pyramids. It must not have taken too long for people to realize that Roman and Egyptian mummies were hardly native to American caves. And some of the "clever" mummy magicians were obviously disappointed.

Mummy Dummy 5: Sideshow Operators

Other mummies have been turned into regular sideshow attractions. For example, a carnival operator named Frank Hansen claimed to have the mummy of a Bigfoot-type creature frozen in a block of ice. Hansen had exhibited the creature in sideshows across the country, but in 1968 he seemed to want respect from the scientific community. He invited two zoologists to examine the block of ice at his farm in Minnesota.

Authors Russell Ciochon, John Olsen, and Jamie James describe what the zoologists saw:

> Its body was hairy and vaguely human, about six feet in height, with long limbs and very large extremities, and it had a simian face with a sloping forehead.

Were they convinced that this was a mummy hoax? Not at all. In fact, they were so certain the creature had once been alive that they asked a curator at the Smithsonian Institution to examine it, but Hansen would not allow this. He later made a plastic model of the mummy for future exhibitions, and the mummy disappeared.

Many people doubt that it was real, but two respected zoologists have publicly stated that it certainly looked real. Were they mummy dummies, too?

Sometimes sideshows used mummies without everyone's knowledge. Imagine the surprise of a television crew when a mummy was found in the darkened fun house at the Nu-Pike Amusement Park in Long Beach, California, on December 7, 1976. Ready to film an episode of *The Six Million Dollar Man*, the director wasn't happy with a dummy hanging from a rope in one part of the fun house, so he asked a crew member to move it. When the man grabbed the dummy, its arm came off — exposing the arm bone of a real mummy.

Authors Christopher Joyce and Eric Stover report that medical examiners and forensic investigators were called to determine who the mummy was and how it had died. They learned that the mummy was a man, and that he had been shot — quite a while ago, it seemed. He died of a .32-caliber gunshot wound; the bullet was old, manufactured between 1830 and 1920. When one medical examiner opened the mummy's mouth for other clues, he was surprised to find a 1924 penny and a ticket from the Museum of Crime in Los Angeles. That ticket and newspaper accounts helped police identify the mummy — a robber known as Elmer McCurdy. Here is his story:

In 1911 McCurdy joined a gang of outlaws. This band robbed a Missouri Pacific train near Coffeyville, Kansas, and then planned to steal a safe carrying over one thousand dollars from another train. On October 6, they stopped a train near Okesa, Oklahoma. But when they opened the safe they discovered that they had robbed the wrong train: only forty-six dollars were inside. A shipment of whiskey improved their spirits. They took it and headed across the Oklahoma wilderness.

Two nights later, McCurdy stopped at a ranch. Drunk and tired, he fell asleep in a hayloft. Soon after, the three-man posse that was tracking him arrived. The trapped McCurdy began firing at the posse. They traded shots for an hour, then all was quiet. A young boy was told to go to the barn to ask McCurdy to surrender. McCurdy refused, reportedly telling the boy, "They can go to the devil." The fighting resumed, and McCurdy was later found dead in the hayloft.

His body was taken to a funeral home in Pawhuska, Oklahoma, but no one knew who McCurdy was. When nobody claimed the corpse, the undertaker embalmed it with arsenic and allowed people to see "The Bandit Who Wouldn't Give Up" for a nickel. Many carnival operators asked to buy the body from the undertaker, but he refused.

ELMER MCCURDY on DISPLAY
"THE MAN WHO WOULDN'T GIVE UP"

Almost five years after McCurdy died, two men from California showed up and claimed that they wanted to take his corpse back to California and give it a proper burial. The body was sent to California — where the two tricksters put it into a carnival sideshow. Eventually, it wound up in the Long Beach fun house.

If you are tempted to think that this is an isolated case, consider the following example. An Australian aborigine named Tambo Tambo was brought to America as a circus performer more than one hundred years ago. On February 23, 1884, he died of pneumonia at the age of twenty-one while on tour with the circus. In 1993, 109 years later, his mummified body was discovered in a Cleveland, Ohio, funeral home. Why had his body been mummified? Why had it been secretly kept? And how much money had been made exhibiting him?

As you can see, there are quite a few ways to make a mummy cry, and each way involves disrespect for the dead. By realizing when mummy dummies are at work, you can help make a mummy happy.

10. Paying Your Respects

Another way to make mummies happy is to visit them respectfully at museums. Locating a museum with a mummy display can take some work. Depending on the type of mummy you want to see — and how much money you want to spend — you may have some success. This chapter describes three trips you might take to see some museums and the mummies they contain. It does not attempt to be comprehensive, nor does it guarantee that these mummies will be on display when you go to visit. Museums are notorious for closing exhibits for years at a time. Before you make plans, check with the museum to see if its mummies will be on display when you arrive.

My suggestions were formed only after extensive reading *and* visits to mummies in North America and Europe, two destinations that are relatively easy and comparatively inexpensive to reach. There are some strange and unusual mummy exhibits to be visited — if not today, sometime in the future.

Mummy Finder: A trip to Egypt?

If you had unlimited money and time, your first and perhaps only destination to view Egyptian mummies would be the Egyptian Museum in Cairo, Egypt. According to many mummy authorities, it contains the finest collection of Egyptian mummies found anywhere in the world. But it was closed in 1980 when Egyptian President Anwar el-Sadat declared that the exhibition of mummies was "against our religious concepts." Eventually Sadat's decision was reversed for two reasons, according to journalist Jamie James. First and foremost, authorities hoped that the reopening of the mummy exhibit would attract more tourists to Egypt. Second, new technology allowed the mummies to be displayed nondestructively. Scientists borrowed an idea from bags of potato chips: just as they are filled with nitrogen to keep the chips fresh, the display cases were filled with nitrogen to prevent fungus and bacteria from growing and destroying the mummy. Finally, in 1994, a new exhibit displaying eleven royal mummies was opened. Eventually, another sixteen mummies will join the display.

MUMMY FINDER: Other fine collections can be found at the Rijksmuseum van Oudheden in Leiden, the Netherlands; the British Museum in London; and the Manchester Museum in Manchester, England.

Even if these foreign destinations aren't in your travel plans for the next few years, you shouldn't have to go too far to find a museum with an Egyptian mummy. In the United States, you'll find any number of Egyptian exhibits. Here are two large ones:

The Field Museum (Chicago). "Inside Ancient Egypt," the museum's permanent exhibit, is housed on two floors and contains almost twenty human mummies of all ages, as well as one bandaged hand and a variety of animal mummies. The exhibit begins in a reconstruction of the Egyptian tomb of Unis-ankh. On the way into the tomb, you pass the mummy of a fifty-year-old woman in a flexed position, covered by a reed mat — an example of an early accidental mummy, about 5,500 years old. Then you wind your way through the tomb and down a circular stairway to the main part of the exhibit, which

has a number of unique features, including four miniature dioramas depicting the mummification process and a large boat which may have been used to carry the mummies of Egyptian royalty. Visitors to Chicago who are interested in mummies should also see the **Oriental Institute** on the campus of the University of Chicago, where an Egyptian mummy is usually exhibited.

Metropolitan Museum of Art (New York City). If you've visited a mummy exhibit in a natural history museum first, you'll notice an immediate difference. As an art museum, the Metropolitan Museum emphasizes the artistic aspects of mummification. That's why you'll see row after row of beautifully decorated mummy cases — and only three actual mummies. One mummy, with a wooden portrait panel over its face, comes from the Roman period, about A.D. 50–100. Another mummy, from 305–30 B.C., has a nicely painted face and feet. But the most interesting mummy is Kharushere, who dates from the Twenty-second Dynasty, or 825–715 B.C. The exhibition of this mummy is quite elaborate and involves the display of Kharushere's four nesting mummy cases: the black outer coffin; the inner coffin with its painted face and blue wig; the innermost coffin, decorated with scenes of Kharushere being presented to Thoth, the god of eternity; and the cartonnage, a kind of papier-mâché form-fitting inner coffin; and finally Kharushere himself. Visitors to New York may also wish to see the Egyptian exhibit at the **Brooklyn Museum.**

MUMMY FINDER: If these museums aren't near your home, you might try to find an Egyptian mummy at one of the following:

Atlanta: Emory University Museum
Baltimore: Walters Art Gallery
Berkeley: Phoebe Hearst Museum of Anthropology
Boston: Museum of Fine Arts
Cincinnati: Cincinnati Art Museum
Denver: Denver Museum of Natural History
Detroit: Detroit Institute of Arts
Kalamazoo: Kalamazoo Public Museum
Memphis: Institute of Egyptian Art and Archaeology
Minneapolis: Minneapolis Institute of Arts
New Haven: Peabody Museum of Natural History
Philadelphia: The University Museum
Pittsburgh: Museum of Art
St. Louis: St. Louis Art Museum
St. Paul: Science Institute of Minnesota
San Diego: Museum of Man
San Francisco: Museum of Fine Arts
San Jose: Rosicrucian Museum

Although most museums have collections that pale in comparison to those in the Field Museum or the Metropolitan Museum, don't make the mistake of believing that a larger collection is necessarily better. A museum with a small mummy exhibit can be fascinating, because more care and attention can be given to it. The Denver Museum of Natural History's mummy display is a case in point.

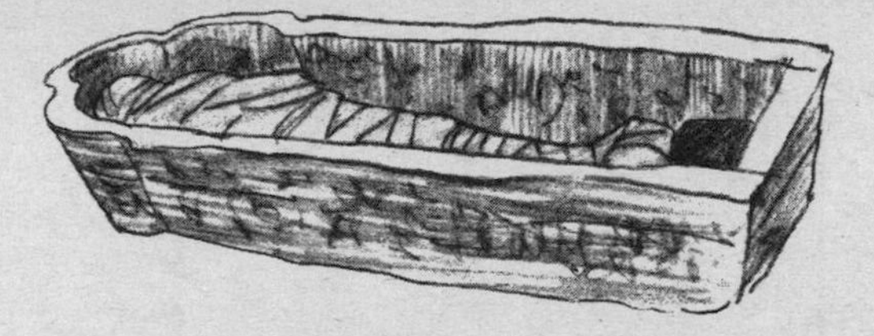

Although the museum has only two mummies, both have mysteries associated with them. One mummy, a woman who died during the Twenty-first Dynasty in Egypt, has puzzled researchers for two reasons. First, an x-ray has revealed a large metal object with an indistinct shape on her abdomen. Researchers would like to find out what it is, but they won't use any destructive techniques. Second, her body was placed in a coffin intended for a man named Mose, or perhaps Moses, both of which were common names at that time in Egypt. Why was a woman's mummy placed in a man's mummy case? Researchers don't have a clue.

Little is known about the second mummy. She died and was mummified sometime during the Nineteenth or the Twentieth Dynasty, close to the time when mummification was at its most skillful. This mummy, though, is a poor example of the mummymaker's craft. Her organs were not removed, and she was wrapped haphazardly. Her mummy looks like a rush job. But why?

MUMMY FINDER: At last visit, the two Egyptian mummies could be found on the third floor of the Denver Museum of Natural History.

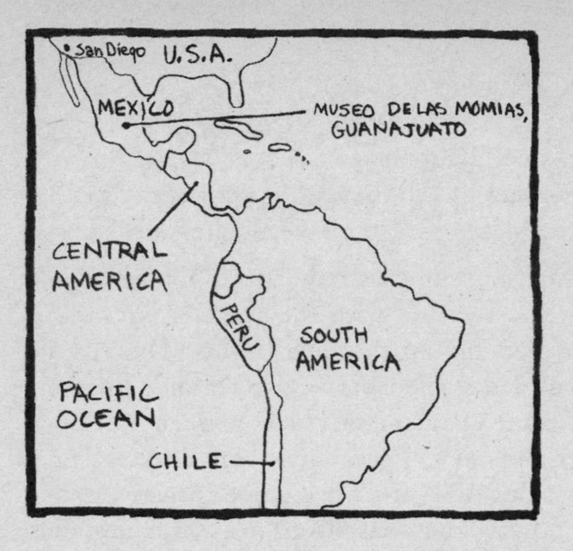

Mummy Finder: A trip to Mexico?

If you're looking for human mummies that are not Egyptian, you'll have to travel a bit further. Except for one Mexican and a number of Peruvian mummies on display at the Museum of Man in San Diego (see Chapter 11), none are on display in this country. You might want to visit South America, where many mummies are exhibited in Peru and Chile. But one of the largest (and definitely among the strangest) mummy museums in the world can be found much closer, in Guanajuato, Mexico.

The **Museo de las momias** is so strange that it takes some getting used to. In seven rooms, this museum displays at least 107 mummified bodies, lying down or propped up, in glass cases. Some are clothed, some aren't. A few are wearing only their socks and/or shoes. Some are old, others are only infants. One tiny baby mummy is labeled "La momia mas pequeña del mundo" — the smallest mummy in the world. Four of the mummies are incomplete; only their heads are on display. Almost all of the mummies are pockmarked with tiny holes where insects have eaten away at the remains.

Most look quite ghoulish. Their jaws have dropped open, and they look as if they were screaming. This is merely an illusion. After people die, their jaw bones often relax, which allows the mouth to open quite naturally.

As you can tell, this museum turns mummies into curiosities at best and freaks at worst. So why does it even exist? And where did so many mummies come from?

Quite simply, from the local cemetery. According to an old law, if a grave had not been paid for after the person in it had been buried for five years, the body was removed. When this first happened, those in attendance as the body was dug up were stunned to find a mummified human body. Because of the dry climate and the soil conditions, mummification occurred quite accidentally and naturally in Guanajuato. Over the years, many bodies were placed on display. Fortunately, the law has been changed and bodies are no longer exhumed for this reason.

Guanajuato's Mummy Museum is a popular tourist spot, and tour buses arrive regularly. Although you may not learn much about mummies or the lives they lived, you will probably learn a great deal about the people who come to visit them.

Mummy Finder: A trip to the bogs?

One of the most fascinating mummy trips you can still take is one to the Netherlands, Germany, and Denmark, where you can see at least fifteen of the world's best bog bodies.

You'll find it easiest to start your trip in Amsterdam. Follow these directions:

1. Head north to Assen. A small town in the northern part of the Netherlands, Assen is the home of the **Drents Museum,** which contains perhaps the most moving display of bog bodies in the world. As you enter the museum, ask for a floor plan and follow it to the far reaches of the second floor in the area labeled "Afdeling Archeologie." On the back wall of this room, near the circular staircase, you will observe images of clouds moving by. And by your feet, you will see a series of bog bodies (called "veenlijken" in Dutch) preserved in flat glass display cases close to the floor.

Picture yourself walking carefully through the bogs on an overcast day. Suddenly you come upon the bodies on

MUMMY FINDER MAP OF A BOG TRIP

1. Drents Museum
2. The Landsmuseum
3. National Museum of Denmark
4. Moesgård Museum
5. Silkeborg Museum

DENMARK
GERMANY
NETHERLANDS
Amsterdam
1. Assen
2. Schleswig
3. Copenhagen
4. Aarbus
5. Silkeborg

the ground. There are four in all, though they are not complete. Two of the bodies (a man and a woman) lie together; their heads are missing, most likely severed by a peat-cutting machine. The man's right arm is cradled under the woman's back, as if to comfort her. Nearby, a third body is covered with a cloth, as if it is sleeping.

Drents Museum
man and woman

Sticking out from the cloth are its head with a swatch of reddish brown hair, the fingers of the right hand, and the toes of both feet; the remainder of the body parts are either missing or in poor condition. Around its neck is a rope noose. Next to that, you see the lower half of another bog body.

Linger a while, contemplating their lives and deaths. Then prepare to move on.

2. Go northeast to Schleswig, Germany. The **Landsmuseum** of the Schloss Gottorf on the outskirts of Schleswig displays an enormous Viking ship in a building known as Nydamhalle. Once you walk past the ship, you reach the farthest room. Here, in large glass display cases set into the walls, are five complete bog bodies ("moorleichen" in German) and one partially preserved head.

The two most famous bodies are known as Windeby I and Windeby II. Windeby is an estate near Schleswig that contains a small bog. In 1952, the owners decided to cut the peat and sell it for fuel. Shortly, workers discovered the body of a fourteen-year-old girl who became known as Windeby I. Although the peat-cutting machinery had already severed one of her legs; a foot, and a hand, work was stopped immediately to study the discovery.

P. V. Glob described the girl's position in the peat:

> She lay on her back, her head twisted to one side, her left arm outstretched. . . . The right arm was bent in against the chest, as if defensively, while the legs were lightly drawn up, the left over the right. The head, with its delicate face, and the hands, were preserved best: the chest had completely disintegrated and the ribs were visible. . . . The hair, reddish from the effects of the bog acids but originally light blond, was of exceptional fineness but had been shaved off with a razor on the left side of the head.

Her eyes were blindfolded with a strip of cloth woven from brown, yellow, and red threads. She had drowned in the first century A.D. and her death was not an accident — her body was anchored by a large stone and branches

from a birch tree. Glob imagined her being "led naked out on to the bog with bandaged eyes . . . and drowned in the little peat pit, which must have held twenty inches of water or more."

A short time after the discovery of Windeby I, a man's body (now known as Windeby II) was found sixteen feet away. Unlike Windeby I, he had been strangled first and then placed in the bog. Sharpened, forked branches had been jammed into the peat around him to make sure that he stayed put.

The three other bodies displayed in separate dioramas are men from Damendorf, Rendswühren, and Dätgen. All are named for the areas where they were discovered and, like Windeby I and II, all were sacrificed. But the most interesting "item" discovered from nearby peat bogs is probably the one from Osterby: a man's head, which was wrapped in a cape made of deerskin. Although peat workers searched for its body, none could be found, and scientists speculate that the Osterby head alone was used as a sacrifice. It has a full head of hair, arranged in an unusual style: one section of hair was twisted and woven into a figure-eight knot — without the use of a fastener.

3. From Schleswig, travel north to Denmark. There, you will be able to visit three museums with bog body displays. First, go to Copenhagen, where the **National Museum of Denmark** exhibits a number of bodies, including three from Borremose. Then, travel to Aarhus on the Jutland peninsula, where the **Moesgård Museum** displays the body of Grauballe Man, who died when he was about thirty-eight years old. Like Lindow Man, he had been hit on the head and his throat had been cut before his body was cast into the bog.

GRAUBALLE MAN

Your tour should rightfully end in Silkeborg, a small town close to Aarhus, where the **Silkeborg Museum** is located. As you may recall, Tollund Man is exhibited there (see Chapter 4). Like the Drents Museum in Assen, where your tour began, the Silkeborg Museum takes great care and shows enormous respect to Tollund Man. On display in a special room, he is in darkness, except when a visitor enters the room. Even when the lights click on, they are not bright. Benches in the room allow a visitor to sit and contemplate his life, almost as if the museum were a religious sanctuary.

Nearby, in another room, is a second bog body, that of Elling Woman, whose body was discovered in 1938. She was hanged about the same time as Tollund Man, somewhere around 200 B.C. Not as well preserved as Tollund Man, she is known for her unusual braided hair.

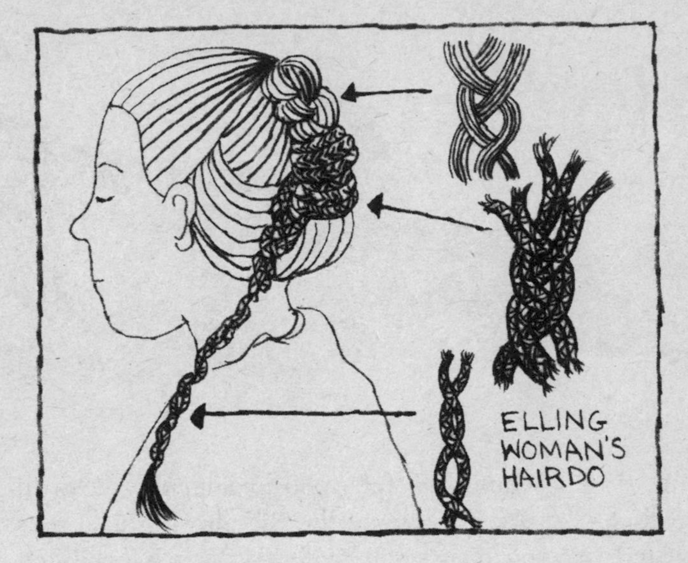

Now that you've taken three mummy trips, you are probably ready to pack your bags or at least check out some more mummy books from your school or local library. If you do decide to meet some mummies, either in person or in print, you may want to keep a record of your encounters. Here's a Mummy Report Form to help you keep track of your mummy memories:

MUMMY REPORT

Name of Mummy:
Location of Mummy Now:
Type of Mummy: ☐ Accidental ☐ Intentional

Date of Mummy:
Mummy's Civilization:

The Mummy's Appearance: [wrappings (if any), face, hair, clothing (if any), and jewelry]

The Condition of the Mummy: [injuries, insect damage, and the amount of mummy (complete or partial) found]

Circumstances (if Known) Surrounding Mummy's Death:

Scientific Analyses Conducted on the Mummy:
Tests: Results:

11. Becoming a Mummy Master

Explore the past while still respecting the dead.
Think about how it would feel to be a mummy.
Think about how it would feel to be on display.
Know how mummies are made.
Know what mummies can tell us.
MUMMY MASTER

In 1966, two teenagers went to Chihuahua, Mexico, in search of mummies. They were intrigued by stories they had heard of mummies found in high caves in northern Mexico, and they wanted nothing more than to have their own mummy. For one month they explored caves in the Sierra Madre Occidental range. Although they found many caves where humans had obviously lived, they did not discover any mummies. Finally they came across a cave, now a shelter for cattle, that showed signs of having been used for human burials. The teenagers found part of a child's mummy near the mouth of the cave. Then they began to dig under the cave's floor.

About two feet below the surface, they found a bundle wrapped in what looked like a mat made from palm tree fronds. According to author Rose Tyson, "The ends of the mat were folded inside 'like an egg roll' and then sewn shut with a vine or fiber cord." Inside, they found the mummified body of a young woman, along with a number of food offerings, such as an ear of corn and some dark berries.

They transported the two mummies to the United States — all without the consent or knowledge of the Mexican or American governments. In the United States, they kept the mummies in a cardboard box, stored in at least three different garages from 1966 to 1980.

Imagine the surprise of a Lemon Grove, California, woman named Elizabeth Whisler on October 17, 1980, when she decided to clean her garage. Without her knowledge, her daughter had allowed two friends to store some belongings there. During the course of her cleaning, she stumbled upon a large carton. When she opened it, she found the body of a naked woman.

Horrified, Whisler telephoned the San Diego police, certain that the body of a murdered woman had been dumped in her garage. The police arrived promptly and, after a cursory examination, added two important facts. First, the woman was a mummy. Second, she wasn't alone in the box. The mummies were turned over to the San Diego Museum of Man while the police searched for the "owners" of the mummies.

Reluctantly, the two men came forward and revealed how they had come into possession of two mummies. Now they wanted to donate them to the Museum of Man in San Diego. Because the mummies had been stolen from Mexico, they did not legally belong to the men. Therefore, the museum had to contact Mexican authorities and request permission to examine them nondestructively. The museum planned a mummy exhibit in which Peruvian and Egyptian mummies would be displayed, and it hoped to be able to display the two Mexican mummies as well. When permission was received, the museum's staff went to work studying the mummies to determine who they were and what had happened to them. Here is what they discovered:

The process of mummification. The mummies were created by natural desiccation; that is, the dry mountain air and the dry conditions in the burial cave caused mummification. This process also may have been helped by the burial methods at the time. After the burial pit was dug, it was lined with pine bark, which was naturally coated with resin. The resin liner may have prevented bacteria from decaying the bodies.

The child. Covered with dirt and dust, the mummy of the child was in a flexed position, but it was incomplete. Portions of its skin, all of its organs, its skull, and its left arm were missing. Still, scientists were able to determine that the mummy was a girl who was approximately one year old at death. They were unable to determine how she died, however.

The young woman. The second mummy was almost intact, except for a missing portion of one foot. It too was in a flexed position, and the skin had dried and hardened. Although the two grave robbers had found her with a full head of black hair, it had begun to deteriorate when the mummy was put into storage. Insects built nests in her hair and ate away at the skin during the fourteen years she had been in garages.

Even so, researchers were able to determine that she had lived between A.D. 1040–1260 and was approximately fifteen years old. X-rays also revealed that she was pregnant at the time of her death. Because the researchers did not want to destroy the body, they could not conclude what caused her death. An analysis of the

MUMMY FINDER: The female mummy is part of the permanent collection of the Museum of Man and is usually on exhibit along with other mummies. Although the museum displays one human and two animal Egyptian mummies, it may be the only museum in the United States to exhibit mummified bodies recovered from Peruvian burial caves; in all, the bodies of four children and one teenager (along with the lower arms of two other children) are exhibited in a re-creation of a cave that exists near Lupo, Peru. The actual cave was looted by grave robbers, and many mummies were thrown over a cliff. In 1913, however, members of the Smithsonian Institution recovered the remaining mummies from the cave; these are the ones now on display. The mummy exhibit can be found on the second floor of the Museum of Man, which is located in Balboa Park near downtown San Diego.

protein content of her hair indicated that she may have been malnourished, and that this may have led to hypertension and a condition known as eclampsia, which brings about premature labor. Without an autopsy, however, researchers will never know for certain.

The two men — whose names have not been made public — were grave robbers in the worst sense. They would have been better off choosing a career that would allow them to work with mummies. If you want to make a mummy happy and become a mummy master one day, there are two fields to consider.

1. Egyptology: Egyptology, the study of the history, archaeology, and language of ancient Egypt, permits a person to research that civilization, which of course includes the subject of mummies.

One prominent Egyptologist, mentioned earlier in the book, is A. Rosalie David. She developed her interest in Egypt — and mummies — at quite an early age:

> When I was six years of age, we had a talk at school . . . and the teacher showed a book with a photograph in it of a reconstruction drawing of three of the pyramids . . . and this visual image really just stirred my imagination, so I knew from then on that I wanted to be an Egyptologist. . . . [My parents] thought it was a phase I would grow out of but I didn't. By the time I was 11 I was reading all the books I could manage on the subject and I knew from that age that that's what I wanted to do.

David also studied Greek and Latin in school, languages that would come in handy when she began to read about ancient Egypt.

Now the Keeper of Egyptology at the Manchester Museum in Manchester, England, David has studied a number of mummies in England and in Egypt. She is particularly interested in studying them because mummies "give us a view of what life was *really* like in ancient Egypt." Despite the glamorous image that films and books often give, ancient Egyptians suffered from all types of ailments and illnesses, and the study of their mummies "balances the picture . . . very well."

Is she ever bothered by examining mummies? No. In fact, she looks upon mummies more as objects rather than people. She explains that the examination team does "refer to them by the name [if it is known]. But I think you do distance yourself from the fact that that actually once was somebody." She admits to being troubled only by the large number of cat mummies that have been found. "I'm very fond of cats," she has said. "I think cat mummies are quite pathetic."

The highlight of her career was the unwrapping and examination of Mummy 1770, which she has described in detail in her book *The Manchester Mummy Project*. "It was the first time it had been done scientifically since 1908," she explains, "and so we felt we really were pioneering this particular investigation." Mummy 1770 is still displayed at the Manchester Museum along with twenty other human mummies from Egypt, including two of children.

2. Physical anthropology. Another way to work with

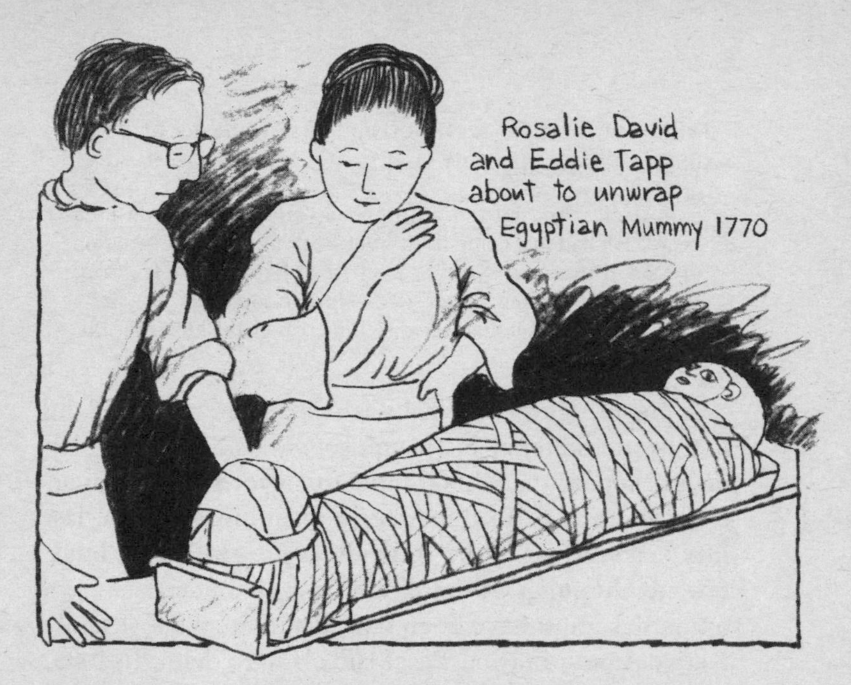
Rosalie David
and Eddie Tapp
about to unwrap
Egyptian Mummy 1770

mummies is to become a physical anthropologist. This entails examining and analyzing human remains and drawing conclusions about them. The work of a physical anthropologist is similar to that of a medical examiner, who conducts autopsies for police departments.

Walter H. Birkby, Curator of Physical Anthropology at the Arizona State Museum, didn't set out to become a physical anthropologist. Although he was always interested in history (especially Neandertal and Cro-Magnon peoples) and science, he planned to be a doctor. However, he got sidetracked when he served in the Korean War and became a dental technician, making false teeth, and later a medical technician. Finally, he went back to college. There, he

> took an elective course in anthropology from some guy in a red beard. He had just come back from working on his dissertation in New Britain [an island that's part of Papua New Guinea]. He could speak pidgin English. He had great stories, and I just couldn't get enough of it. Ultimately, I decided that this was for me.

In his present job, Birkby is responsible for all of the prehistoric material in the museum's collection, which includes more than 3,000 individuals recovered from archaeological digs in the American southwest in the last fifty years. Most of the individuals are skeletons, but a few are mummies. Although the museum once had more mummies, most have been repatriated to groups (usually Native American tribes) that laid claim to them. In 1993, only eleven Native American mummies were part of the museum's collection, but they were no longer on display. Eventually, they too will be repatriated.

Like some anthropologists, Birkby is concerned that the possibility of exploring the past will be lost if all mummies are repatriated and buried. People, he feels,

> don't know what a mummy looks like [or] how important they are for [the] information you can get from them. It's more than just a skeleton, there's tissue there, there's certain [information] you'd only see by having that intact individual.

This is a somewhat controversial opinion, since some other anthropologists believe it is important not to display human remains — no matter what type of information is lost.

Perhaps you, too, will decide to become a mummy master and take up the study of physical anthropology, Egyptology, or even archaeology. Until then, you can consider what a mummy might say if it really could talk to you:

Keep in mind that most mummies would be quite surprised if they only knew what had happened to them.

When a mummy is taken from a tomb (or a cave or a bog), it has been removed from its burial place — often with good intentions. Sometimes this is to make sure that grave robbers don't destroy the mummy. Other times, this is done because the mummy is an interesting or unusual specimen. More often, perhaps, a mummy is retrieved so that it can be studied.

Without question, the examination of mummies helps us understand the history of the earth and its people. Researchers can learn important facts about past civilizations that can educate and help us in the present.

But what to do with mummies after they are studied raises many concerns. Should they be displayed in museums at all? Or should only certain types of mummies be displayed? By carefully selecting and respectfully displaying a few mummies, researchers can show people how life was lived in the past and how other civilizations dealt with the subject of death.

But creating a respectful display is a difficult task. Visiting a mummy in a museum should be similar to attending a funeral and viewing the deceased person in a casket. Mummies placed in tasteful, instructive exhibits, such as natural-looking dioramas, can honor the dead. However, mummies put in Lucite boxes in the center of the museum floor under bright lights (as some occasionally are) show little respect. And the same is true perhaps when detached arms or sandaled feet are exhibited.

Remember that even when a mummy is displayed

thoughtfully by a museum, it is still not allowed to have its final rest. So the next time you see a mummy, ask yourself how you'd feel about having your own mummified body on exhibit centuries from now. Then wonder how the person who was that mummy might have felt. Becoming a mummy master means not only that you understand how mummies were made and how they can share their secrets, but that you understand how to balance your desire to explore the past with your need to respect the dead. That's the most important challenge mummy masters face, and one that does not have an easy resolution.

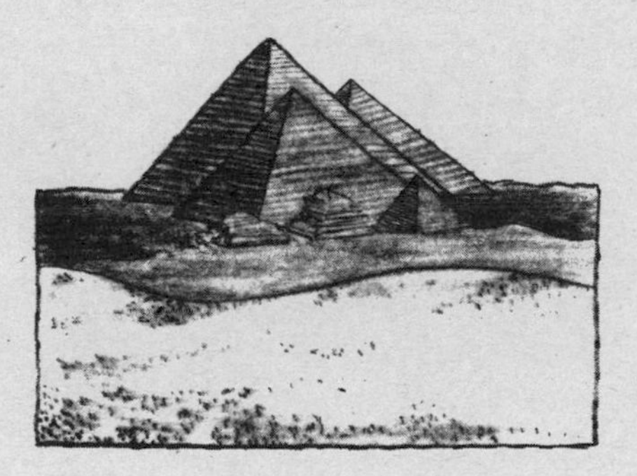

Acknowledgments and Bibliography

My own search for mummies involved more than two years of investigation and many visits to museums throughout the United States and Europe. I especially wish to thank A. Rosalie David of the Manchester Museum and Walter Birkby of the Arizona State Museum for their contributions to this book. I am also appreciative of the kindness shown by Luis Cuevas of John Jay College of Criminal Justice, for assistance with Spanish translations; Craig Wilkie, volunteer worker at the Denver Museum of Natural History; and Dr. Marcia Brontman, who took me on a mummy tour of Chicago.

I consulted the following works in writing this book. Wherever possible, I have cited the author whose work I referred to. Those marked by an asterisk (*) are suitable for younger readers.

Adams, Barbara. *Egyptian Mummies.* Second edition. Aylesbury, England: Shire Publications, 1988. Reprinted 1992.

*Andrews, Carol. *Egyptian Mummies.* London: British Museum Publications, 1984.

*Beattie, Owen, and John Geiger. *Buried in Ice*. London: Hodder and Stoughton, 1992.

———. *Frozen in Time*. New York: Dutton, 1987.

*Berrill, Margaret. *Mummies, Masks and Mourners*. London: Evans Brothers, 1989.

Besom, Thomas. "Another Mummy." *Natural History*, April 1991, 66–67.

Brothwell, Don. *The Bog Man and the Archaeology of People*. Cambridge: Harvard University Press, 1986.

Budge, E. A. Wallis. *The Mummy*. 1925. Reprint. New York: Outlet Books, 1989.

Ciochon, Russell, John Olsen, and Jamie James. *Other Origins*. New York: Bantam Books, 1990.

Cockburn, Aidan, and Eve Cockburn. *Mummies, Disease and Ancient Cultures*. Abridged edition. New York: Cambridge University Press, 1983.

Coles, Bryony, and John Coles. *People of the Wetlands*. London: Thames and Hudson, 1989.

David, A. Rosalie (ed.). *Mysteries of the Mummies*. New York: Scribner's, 1978.

David, A. Rosalie, and E. Tapp (eds.). *Evidence Embalmed: Modern Medicine and the Mummies of Ancient Egypt*. Dover, N.H.: Manchester University Press, 1984.

———. *The Mummy's Tale*. London: Michael O'Mara Books, 1992.

El Mahdy, Christine. *Mummies, Myth and Magic*. London: Thames and Hudson, 1989.

Fagan, Brian. *New Treasures of the Past*. Leicester, England: Windward, 1987.

Frayling, Christopher. *The Face of Tutankhamun*. Boston: Faber and Faber, 1992.

Fowler, Brenda. "Scientists Enthralled by Bronze Age Body." *New York Times*, October 1, 1991, p. C1.

George, Angelo (ed.) *Prehistoric Mummies from the Mammoth Cave Area*. Louisville, KY: George Publishing Company, 1990.

Glob, P. V. *The Bog People*. Translated by Rupert Bruce-Mitford. Boston: Faber and Faber, 1969.

Guthrie, R. Dale. *Frozen Fauna of the Mammoth Steppe: The Story of Blue Babe*. Chicago: University of Chicago Press, 1990.

Hart Hansen, Jens Peter, Jorgen Meldgard, and Jorgen Nordquist (eds.). *The Greenland Mummies*. London: British Museum Publications, 1991.

Haury, Emil W. *The Stratigraphy and Archaeology of Ventana Cave*. 1950. Reprint. Tucson: University of Arizona Press, 1975.

Hochschild, Adam. "The Secret of a Siberian River Bank." *New York Times Magazine*, March 28, 1993, 29–31.

James, Jamie. "Taking a Cue from the Lowly Potato Chip Bag." *New York Times*, March 6, 1994, sec 2, 40.

Jordan, Paul. *The Face of the Past*. London: B. T. Batsford, 1984.

Joyce, Christopher, and Eric Stover. *Witnesses from the Grave*. New York: Ballantine, 1991.

*Lauber, Patricia. *Tales Mummies Tell*. New York: Crowell, 1985.

Kenyon, Denise. *Lindow Man: His Life and Times*. Manchester, England: Manchester Museum, 1991.

Malek, Jaromir. *The Cat in Ancient Egypt*. London: British Museum Press, 1993.

McHargue, Georgess. *Mummies*. Philadelphia: Lippincott, 1972.

Meloy, Harold. *Mummies of Mammoth Cave*. Shelbyville, IN: Micron Publishing Company, 1993.

Moseley, Michael E. *The Incas and Their Ancestors*. New York: Thames and Hudson, 1992.

Norman, Bruce. *Footsteps: Nine Archaeological Journeys of Romance and Discovery*. London: BBC Books, 1987.

*Perl, Lila. *Mummies, Tombs, and Treasures*. New York: Clarion, 1987.

Pettigrew, Thomas J. *A History of Egyptian Mummies*. 1934. Reprint. Los Angeles: North American Archives, n.d.

Reeves, Nicholas. *The Complete Tutankhamun*. New York: Thames and Hudson, 1990.

Roberts, David. "The Iceman: Lone Voyager from the Copper Age." *National Geographic,* June 1993, 36–67.

———. " 'Reverse Archaeologists' Are Tracing the Footsteps of a Cowboy-Explorer." *Smithsonian,* December 1993, 28–38.

Ross, Anne, and Don Robins. *The Life and Death of a Druid Prince.* London: Rider, 1989.

Ryan, Donald P. "Exploring the Valley of the Kings." *Archaeology,* January/February 1994, 52–59.

Schobinger, Juan. "Sacrifices of the High Andes." *Natural History,* April 1991, 62–68.

Sjøvold, Torstein. "Frost and Found." *Natural History,* April 1993, 60–63.

Smith, G. Elliott, and Warren R. Dawson. *Egyptian Mummies.* 1924. Reprint. London: Kegan Paul, 1991.

Spencer, A. J. *Death in Ancient Egypt.* Harmondsworth, England: Penguin, 1982.

Spindler, Konrad. *The Man In the Ice.* (London: Weidenfeld and Nicholson, 1994.

Stead, I. M., J. B. Bourke, and Don Brothwell. *Lindow Man: The Body in the Bog.* London: British Museum Publications, 1986.

Tyson, Rose A., and Daniel V. Elerick (eds.). *Two Mummies from Chihuahua, Mexico: A Multidisciplinary Study.* San Diego: San Diego Museum of Man, 1985.

Ubelaker, Douglas, and Henry Scammell. *Bones: A Forensic Detective's Casebook.* New York: HarperCollins, 1992.

van der Sanden, E. A. B. (ed.). *Mens en moeras.* Assen, Holland: Drents Museum, 1990.

*Vornholt, John. *Mummies.* New York: Avon, 1991.

Wetherill, Benjamin Alfred. *The Wetherills of Mesa Verde.* Lincoln: University of Nebraska Press, 1987.

*Wilcox, Charlotte. *Mummies and Their Mysteries.* Minneapolis: Carolrhoda Books, 1993.

Index

Pot from
Peruvian
grave